AF552528

The Unspoken Curse

The Unspoken Curse

V. K. Madhavan Kutty

Translated from Malayalam by
Prema Jayakumar

tara press, new delhi

Tara Press
(Trade division of India Research Press)
B-4/22, Safdarjung Enclave, New Delhi – 110 029.
Ph.: 24694610; Fax : 24618637
www.indiaresearchpress.com
contact@indiaresearchpress.com; bahrisons@vsnl.com

2005

ISBN : 81-87943- 84-X

Work of Fictional Writing

Cataloging in Publication Data

V K Madhavan Kutty
The Unspoken Curse

1. Fiction - Indian. 2. Contemporary - Women 3. Kerala.
I. Title. II. Author

Printed in India at Focus Impressions, New Delhi – 110 003.

One

Kalyanikutty Edathi was dead. I found out about this when I reached the flat from the office.

The postman had pushed in an inland letter under the locked door. I could make out that the letter which lay there was from home. The handwriting looked familiar. The only people who wrote regularly were Kalyanikutty Edathi and Kumarettan. Kumarettan wrote mostly about what was happening in the village. Kalyanikutty Edathi wrote only about what happened in the house.

I thought I'd read the letter later. I had a wash and came into the room planning to spend some time dreaming about Jyothi who worked with me. I'd been feeling for some time that Jyothi's playfulness was getting to be a little too much. Most days I felt that other colleagues were noting her behaviour.

When Jyothi came to my table and went away, the others in the office would look at each other and exchange meaningful smiles. When she left, Daljit Singh would ask again, 'Kya ho raha hai, bhai?'

She came as though she needed to ask doubts about the meaning, or spelling or use of some word or the other. But I'd started having doubts about the meaning behind all that for some time now. Even if I remained quite serious, she would smile and flirt. Though Jyothi was good-looking I had never felt attracted towards her. It was not because Parvathi waited for me at home. I've always wondered why Jyothi did not understand what I felt about her. My colleagues had always been surprised at my lack of reaction. I'd never thought about why I felt so indifferent towards her. My friend Chidambaram always said she'd take advantage of me if I did not bridle her. Others would just say she wasn't bad.

One day, quite unexpectedly, Jyothi invited me to dinner. And that, at a big hotel in the city. I first said, 'I'll tell you tomorrow.' I did not feel like saying no immediately. I needed to discuss the matter, with my own mind.

I opened the letter as I lay there wondering whether to go for dinner with Jyothi or not. It was Kumarettan's handwriting. Small, regular writing. 'Kalyanikutty Edathi is dead.'

I felt guilty about not having opened the letter as soon as I got back from the office. I sat for a while without moving. My thoughts were rushing to the village. 'The mango tree to the east of the house has been cut down...'Kumarettan's letter continued. The mango tree had grown very old. They say that it was planted when Koman Nair was the Karyakkar. It had stopped bearing long ago. 'The yam which had been planted in the piece of land next to the temple yielded nothing this year.'

'Pottekkat Nanu Nair died last Friday.' All of us called him Pavam Nanu Nair or Poor Nanu Nair. Narayanan Nair was one of those men who are central to a village. He had not married. We had heard rumours of a relationship somewhere at Mankara. Once in a while Nanu Nair would vanish for a couple of days. 'He must have gone to see the woman,' everyone believed.

Nanu Nair had not got married because his family had insisted that he marry his uncle's daughter.

Kumarettan also had not got married because his uncle's daughter Visalakshi whom he was supposed to marry was cross-eyed. The family had disapproved of his stand that he would not marry the girl he was supposed to marry only because she had cross-eyes. 'So what if her eyes are a little awry. Her complexion is so good she looks as though blood would burst out of the skin if you just touch it. 'If they're so particular I should marry her, I won't get married at all,' Kumarettan decided. After a while, Visalakshi got married. She was with her husband at Pune. She would not meet

Kumarettan when she came home. She wouldn't come out on to the veranda when Kumarettan came to the house. Both Kumarettan and Visalakshi had no regrets about not getting married to each other. Visalakshi thought that it was by luck that she was able to marry Raghavan from the next village. Kumarettan had an awful temper.

Though she was cross eyed, Kumarettan had once tried to get closer to Visalakshi. Visalakshi was bathing in the pond near the house. She dipped her head into the water and straightened throwing her hair back and there stood Kumarettan on the steps. She could make out from his look what his intentions were. Kumarettan could still remember her look as she said, 'Don't you dare touch me!'. He had not thought that the girl intended to be his bride would be so impudent. His attitude was that he had only tried to touch what he was entitled to. He had decided that day that he did not want a cross eyed or cross mouthed female for a wife. The family did not know of this incident. If Visalakshi's father had come to know of it he would not have let his daughter and nephew go free like this. Perhaps he would have got them married by force. But this attempt by Kumarettan at the side of the pond lay asleep on the steps of the pond. It stayed a chapter that remained for ever closed in both their minds.

I finished reading Kumarettan's letter after I finished cooking.

'It was all over very quickly. She was cremated in the northern compound. Sankaranarayanan could not reach in time. Anyway, he's not particularly bothered about his mother. I've written to him as well. I know that you will also find it difficult to come from such a distance.' It was clear from Kumarettan's letter that no one had waited for me. Even Sankaranarayanan was informed only by letter. They must have thought that Kalyanikutty Edathi's death warranted only that much interest. They would have been in a hurry to inter her body. The telegraph office was not all that far from the house. No one would even have thought of going to the public call office near by. They had written to inform people concerned about her death – it mattered only that much to them, that was all the importance they had given to it.

I sat for some time holding Kumarettan's letter in my hand. I was unaware of the time. The letter had been written on Friday. It was Tuesday today. Letters posted in the post-box on the road, very often did not reach the addressee at all. Luckily this had reached me. Or I would not even have known that Kalyanikutty Edathi had died.

There was a telephone in one of the houses nearby. Should I ring up and tell Kumarettan that I would not be able to go? He would just say that it did not matter. It was after all Kalyanikutty Edathi who had died.

'It was all over soon. She did not trouble anybody.' He would have meant that no one had to do anything for her. If

Kalyanikutty Edathi had fallen ill and had to stay in bed all of them would have prayed that it should be over soon. And death would have come in a rush in response to their prayers. Anyway, Kalyanikutty Edathi had gone away without troubling anyone. These people would not have said she was lucky to have gone like that; they would have said it was their luck. He had not written any details. Perhaps because the death had been sudden.

Kumarettan knew the number of the telephone in the house nearby. And there was a telephone in the house next door in the village. But Kumarettan would not go to that house. He had slapped Naniamma's son one day. The reason was a family squabble. Kumarettan had beaten him because he had been impudent. 'What right has that man to beat my son?' asked Naniamma. But there was another telephone a couple of houses away. But he would have decided that a telephone call or a telegram was not needed to inform me of Kalyanikutty Edathi's death, an ordinary inland letter was plenty. I could not understand how Kumarettan could be like this. Kalyanikutty Edathi had taken so much trouble for Kumarettan. But it was always like that when something concerned Kalyanikutty Edathi. All of them were alike in that.

No one would have mourned Kalyanikutty Edathi. Everyone needed her services. Still no one would say, 'If only she had been alive.' Even her soul would not regret the fact that no one mourned her. Kalyanikutty Edathi was just a machine that worked in the tharavad. You could repair it if it broke down. Or you could throw it away. That was everyone's attitude to Kalyanikutty Edathi.

Kalyanikutty Edathi was a character not wanted by anyone, not loved by anyone, someone on whom all blame could be laid, someone to whom all faults could be attributed. She had never known what it was to be loved, she had never experienced sympathy.

Everyone thought that she was just a machine that could work non-stop for twenty four hours. No one cared to find out how she was.

I laid down Kumarettan's letter. There was nothing in it which merited keeping. Who could I complain to? I wondered if I was also one of the creatures who had been cast out of the inner circle. I folded the inland latter and kept it in a book. Why? There were plenty of memories folded and kept in my mind. Memories which would not fade away. All of them about Kalyanikutty Edathi.

Two

Why had they cremated Kalyanikutty Edathi in the northern compound? The other compound near the house had been taken over by the committee in charge of the renovation of the temple. That compound was right next to the temple. One could not cremate dead bodies there. Our village does not have any public place where bodies can be cremated. Each family had to use its own property for cremation or burial.

Our ancestors had been cremated near the river. The family must have decided that Kalyanikutty Edathi did not deserve a place there. The mango tree to the east of the house must have been chosen to accompany her because it did not bear fruits. Nothing would grow under it either. Still, they must have regretted having to cut it down for this. Timber merchant Ahmed Rauther had looked at it and named a good price for it.

People had been cremated near the river because it was believed that the souls of those cremated on the banks of the river Nila would attain salvation. But one had to walk two miles to reach there. When it came to Kalyanikutty Edathi, the eternal salvation of her soul would have taken second place to the convenience of the others. The family would have been sad about having to cut down the mango tree to the east of the house. Kumarettan had not written why Kalyanikutty Edathi had not been cremated on the banks of the river. Why had they gone against the convention in Kalyanikutty Edathi's case? He must have avoided writing for the salvation of his own soul. Why make people say that he had done something that he should not have?

There had been no deaths in the family since Amma and Cheriamma died. Ammaman had died in his wife's house. He would not have regretted the fact that he could not die in his own house. His wife and children had looked after him so well. He had wished to with them all the time. He would have been happy that death came when he was at his wife's place.

But as he grew older Ammaman became more attached to his natal home. The feeling that this was the house of his birth strengthened in him. He did not even think of asking for his share of the family property. His wife and children were also not interested in grabbing that share. Their attitude was that god had given them enough to live comfortably on and that was enough. Ammaman could not even think of the tharavad being partitioned into four and six pieces. But it was only natural that he loved his children more than he loved his nephews and nieces. Muthassi would say, 'He can't bear to spend even an hour away from her. But he does come running whenever anything happens here, you've got to admit that.' Once a month, and then on any special day, Ammaman would come to the tharavad.

Far away, in Ammaman's wife's place at Ponnani, they did not cremate bodies as they did in our place. They followed a different system. The soil in their compound contained more sand and was not as sticky as the soil in our place. It was good for coconut trees. There, they made flat cakes of dried cowdung and covered the body with a number of them, forming an oven. Before setting fire to the whole, they would pour a lot of ghee into the furnace and put a piece of sandalwood. It was much cheaper than burning a body the conventional way with firewood. It was not that the family didn't know that when they cremated Kalyanikutty Edathi the usual way. They must have been worried about the comments that would have come from the village if they departed from the usual method.

One day Ammaman had come storming into the house. He hung up his umbrella in the ring on the veranda and dragged Ettan by his arm. 'So your impudence has reached this far, has it?'

he asked as he beat him. Ammaman appeared to have lost his senses from anger. 'Just because you have some brains, you think you can do anything. Do you plan to send all of us to the gallows?' Everyone stood around watching the beating go on. Even my mother did not have the courage to stop her brother and ask him what the beating was for. No one was allowed to question the Karanavar's right to punish his nephews. No one had the courage to ask that demonic figure to stop. The young children who were at home stood behind doors and shivered. The women were struck dumb.

Finally, uncle got fed up of beating Ettan and yelling at him and ordered, 'Bring me some water, don't stand around.' It was Kalyanikutty Edathi who brought the water. It was as though she would also be beaten if she did not bring the water immediately. No one else even thought of bringing the water.

Ettan had received a real beating. From the way he went about it, it looked as though Ammaman had taken lessons from the police. The crime was that Ettan had created a crossword puzzle and sent it to a newspaper to be published. He had also written underneath it that anyone who completed it correctly would get a good prize. The completed answers were to be sent to the address of the tharavad within the 15th of the next month. No one knew how Ammaman had got to know of all this. Since Ettan was first in his class in all subjects some of his jealous classmates must have sneaked on him. There was no attempt to ask if the accusation was true and no chance for Ettan to say, 'I only wrote it out, it is still in my desk.' Uncle's temper had not allowed the time for all that.

Ettan went in. We didn't dare go near him. After a while my mother came out with a glass of tea and asked her brother, 'What happened to you?' It was only then that he seemed to come down to earth. Amma did not question the right of the uncle to punish his nephew. That was one of the facts of life of the matrilineal system. Ammaman came and sat on the easy chair in the veranda with his legs stretched out. When he cooled down a little, one could see a kind of helplessness on his face, as though he could not decide what to say and to whom, how to start on an explanation. He must have regretted what he did. His sitting alone like that without speaking to anyone meant that. He must have been thinking of the lunacy he had displayed and apologising to himself. An uncle could not ask his nephew's pardon. He had to find peace by expressing his regrets to himself. He could not even say before others that he should not have done that.

He drank the tea and heaved a big sigh and came back to his surroundings. The house where even footsteps had not been heard since his arrival slowly came back to normal.

In the confrontation caused by Uncle's lack of patience to enquire into the truth of an accusation and his uncontrollable temper on one side and

Ettan's innocence of any wrongdoing, Ammaman did not win. Neither did Ettan lose. When the victory and defeat of that confrontation were weighed up, both sides could only regret what had happened. Uncle came to his senses only when he had exorcised his temper through the beating he had given his nephew. The thought that he was an uncle and had done this must have troubled him and this must have persuaded him to buy Ettan a shirt the next time he came home. To avoid any comment, he brought me one too. Everyone was aware of a sense of regret behind all this.

Ammaman sat in the easy chair and said, 'Give him something to eat'. And then looked towards the room and said, 'Don't get into things you'll regret.' One could make out that what you'll regret meant what you don't understand. Anger was giving way to advice. Ettan who had been punished for a crime he had not committed was silent. No one dared to minister to his swollen face or to ask if the punishment had not been too severe.

Finally it was Kalyanikutty Edathi who gave Ettan a towel and told him to go and have a bath in the pond. By now the time was four o'clock in the evening. But it was only by mealtime that night that the house went back to normalcy.

Three

Raman Nair took care of all the affairs of the tharavad. He was a like a karyasthan, a manager. As there were no grown men staying there at the time, he felt he had to take care of things. He lived in his house with his elder sister Panchaliamma. Her life consisted of cooking two meals for her brother, doing the rest of the housework as fast as possinble and going to the temple twice a day. If she had time, she would, once in a while, go to a neighbouring house and sit there and talk. She would hear all the latest scandals from there. But she would have no part in spreading them.

Raman Nair would go to his wife's place only once a month. This was two miles away. He did not have any children. If you asked him about children, he would say, 'I don't have any such problem.' Gopalan once said that it was not that he didn't have them, but couldn't have them. If he was asked further questions he would just laugh. And then add, 'It's not her fault.' Raman Nair's wife's people had enough to live on. He would go and stay there for three or four days. After that he would feel awkward about staying there. No one could predict when Raman Nair would go to his wife's place and when he would come back. When he set out to visit his wife, no one would ask him when he would be back. When he returned from there, the people there would also not ask him when he would come next. There was no place for questions in that marriage. A contented life which wandered between his own house and his wife's house. He would say softly once in a while, 'I'm going to Kunhilakshmi's house. I'll be back in a few days.' Panchaliamma had never stopped him.

It must have been Raman Nair who decided which mango tree had to be cut down to burn Kalyanikutty Edathi's body. He would normally assert his importance on such occasions. His attitude was, 'All this is my right.' On ordinary days, he would come to our place at some time during the day and sit on the bench in the verandah. He would sit there and talk for a while. That was how we came to know all the happenings in the neighbourhood. And each incident would be accompanied by Raman Nair's explanations. 'They say Rajalaskshmi's husband does not come very regularly these days. He has another woman at Kunnathur. I also heard that he does not come because he has leukoderma. Who knows all this, Guruvayoorappa! That Korath Achuthan Nair said he was a clerk in the court, didn't he? He is the Ameen. He goes regularly to his wife's place, but won't give her any money for expenses.' We knew all these stories from Raman Nair. Quite a few of us believed that Raman Nair would not lie.

'You should watch Raman Nair act the karyasthan,' Gopalan would say, 'He thinks no end of himself. If you see him walk around with his chest thrust out and the upper body bent backwards, you can be sure, he has some special task on hand. It might be a wedding, it might be looking after things in a house where there had been a recent death, anything like that. He's a real sharp file.' Raman Nair would look after the affairs of households belonging to kiriyath nairs only, no household of a caste lower than that could hope for his help.

Raman Nair always drank a glass of tea when he came home. The tea had to be strong and had to be served in a glass tumbler. Once when he was given the tea in a cup, he poured the tea into the saucer and drank from the saucer. Gopiettan laughed, 'You are supposed to drink from the cup.'

'What are you saying, child? All that is for the white man. Why do you need this thing at all?' Why does a cup need a handle? Gopiettan laughed and went inside.

Raman Nair would visit only the houses of Nairs. When you walked home from the Post Office, you had to pass a two-storeyed house. It was called 'Kottaram', the palace. Gopalan said, 'He must be trying to tell us he is of royal blood!' Raman Nair was of the opinion that just because he had gone to Singapore and made some money we did not have to bow before him. 'Why did that nasrani build his palace here among the nair households? Couldn't he go somewhere else. There are a few nairs here in this area who have been won over by Abraham's money. All of them are the type who just want to down a couple of free drinks every night. I don't want anything of his.'

Abraham had returned from Singapore and settled down beside the Nila to live quietly. Only Abraham and his wife stayed in the house. Both his children were still in Singapore. A boy and a girl. The boy married an American who worked in a private company at Singapore. They had regretted the fact that they did not get the dowry they might have, if the boy had married a Malayali Christian girl. However, when, after a few years, when he tried to get his father and mother to go to Singapore, that regret vanished. When the young couple were about to return to Singapore after the first visit, Christina had told Abraham, 'Daddy, you and mummy must come and stay with us for some time.' This got rid of all their regrets about dowry. 'After some years, we shall go and stay with them permanently,' Abraham used to say. The distance from Raman Nair to Abraham who drank every evening and dreamt of Singapore and his dutiful daughter-in-law Christina, was a long one.

Another house that Raman Nair did not visit was that of Bhageerathi Amma. When they were both young, one day, Raman Nair had been returning from the market when he saw Bhageerathi Amma come from the temple pond, wearing just a mundu, a towel flung over her breasts and hair falling over her back. Raman Nair remembered a few lines of a poem which described wet hair cascading over the buttocks of a young woman. Though he was not a poetic man normally, he had been involved in some pranks at that time.

When Bhageerathi passed him, Raman Nair took his fill. And then stood and looked some more. He cleared his throat as well. Bhageerathi went home and complained to her uncle, 'Raman's getting a little free.' There was mattering in the house. Her people said, 'This isn't good. But you knew he was standing and staring at you only because you turned around, right?' Her uncle was of the opinion that both of them had been at fault. The uncle too had spent time near the pond in his youth. Anyway, the people of the village had one more piece of gossip to chew over. From that day onwards Bhageerathi and Raman avoided each other even at the door of the temple. The old days when they had gone to school together and Raman had helped Bhageerathi with her sums became just memories. Still, wasn't it natural to look at an old friend when you met her in that costume? The fact that he had not done anything beyond that consoled Raman Nair. Though Bhageerathi grew up and got married and went away, Raman Nair could not forget her betrayal.

'Would you have married her?' Gopalan had asked once. The reply was, 'Impudent brat'.

It was Raman Nair who decided which mango tree should be cut down, on which day the ceremony of collecting bones should be, at what time and so on. Till the feast on the sixteenth day, Raman Nair would come in the morning and evening. He was very busy on those days. Since there weren't any grown up men at home, all this had to be looked after by him, his attitude seemed to say. A covered space had to be set aside for the ceremonies, everything had to be prepared for the feast on the sixteenth day, the cleansing of the household after that had to be arranged. Raman Nair did not like anyone else interfering in all this. He was very particular that the power that was temporarily in his hands, or the responsibility that he had taken on should be his alone to deal with properly.

All this time he would stand in a peculiarly indecent pose, holding the two corners of the mundu with one hand, just below his stomach, as though he was scared something would fall off. That picture from my childhood still remained clear in my mind.

People who came on condolence visits would talk about the dear-departed's good qualities usually. Though her family had only recognised Kalyanikutty Edathi's bad qualities so far, they would have pretended in respect of conventions. However, the neighbours and relatives who came would not speak too much about Kalyanikutty Edathi's qualities. They would be afraid that the family would not like it. One doesn't go on a condolence visit to earn the bereaved family's displeasure. Raman Nair would also engage in other duties at that time to avoid any awkwardness.

There was an atmosphere of relief rather than grief in the house at that time. Those who had to die, died. Everybody had to die, that was something that could not be prevented. It was difficult to say that that was the reason for the relief. Where Kalyanikutty Edathi was concerned, no one thought of such philosophical issues. It would be just relief that it was all over. Convention demanded that a minimum of ceremonies had to be performed. They would do those in fear of what the people would say. The decision to cut down the mango tree would also be because they were afraid of public opinion.

That mango tree had been like a senior member of the household. It had been planted by my great-grandfather Koppan Nair. It was shade and fortune for the household. When she walked below it, Muthassi would pray, 'Guruvayurappa, take care of me.' The members of the tharavad believed that it was Koppammaman who took care of the tharavad even these days. Muthassi would warn us to be careful because Koppammaman kept an eye on everything even now. So, there were more expressions of regret regarding the demise of the mango tree. Still, it was sensible to cut that particular mango tree. It was barren. Kalyanikutty Edathi had also not had children for a long time. Everyone had believed that she was barren. She had a child at the age of thirty seven. That must have been why they chose that mango tree.

As they waited to cremate Kalyanikutty Edathi's body, there was more praise for the mango tree. They must have been praying for the eternal rest of the tree. At least some of them would have felt that there had been a killing for the sake of one dead being. It was not that they loved nature or regretted cutting down a tree, but that they disliked the person for whose sake it was done.

Till the days of the pula were over and the final sixteenth day feast, Raman Nair would not have anything to eat from the house. He would chew elaborately with tobacco for accompaniment. He would spit accurately at the bed of the banana tree without letting a drop fall in the yard. The children in the household would say when they watched Raman Nair walk towards the house, 'There he comes to chew betel leaves.'

Kumarettan had written only that it was all over very soon. What had been the trouble with Kalyanikutty Edathi, had she been bedridden, he had not written any of the details. Did his words show relief that she had not troubled anyone? He must have felt that that was all that anyone needed to know. Muthassi had been bedridden for a year after a stroke. Every morning she had to be given a sponge-bath with a wet towel to prevent bed sores being formed. You had to bow before the affection and care that went into that nursing. Just as well that Kalyanikutty Edathi did not have to spend time in bed. Wonder what these people would have done if she had had to. It does not bear thinking. The machine called Kalyanikutty Edathi had stopped functioning.

Kumarettan at least should have seen her differently from the others. 'Kalyani fill that big vessel with some water. Let me have a bath,' Kumarettan would call out on the days when he came late. The orders were always addressed to Kalyanikutty Edathi. The two other sisters were not used to working hard. And the attitude of the family was, let Kalyanikutty do all the work. If she was five minutes late with the hot water the comment would be that it would probably be the next morning by the time one was able to bathe. The fire had to be made up again, blown into flames and the water heated. Before that ten or fifteen buckets of water had to be drawn up from the well. No one was bothered by all that trouble. How many times had we seen Kalyanikutty Edathi sit before the fire rubbing her eyes with the edge of her mundu as the smoke got into them and made them water.

Kumarettan's clothes had to be washed by Kalyanikutty Edathi every day. Saudamini who was elder to

Kalyanikutty Edathi and Vanaja were exempt from this duty on the excuse 'both of them can't touch washing soap, they start itching and burning'. Narayani who came to sweep and clean was almost a part of the family. She too took her cue from the family where behaviour to Kalyanikutty Edathi was concerned. All the same the family took great pleasure in narrating the scandals about her. They said she had tried to kill herself by jumping into the well soon after she completed her tenth standard. The fourth month after her periods started they had stopped. The midwife Kunhikutti Amma had come and cleared up the trouble. Kumarettan had also come under suspicion as the author of the trouble. That was perhaps why the stories about Narayani stayed within the bounds of the inner courtyard.

There was no point in rushing to the village now. They would only ask why I had spent so much money and gone there. They would only think that the money would have been better utilised in repairing the northern veranda of the house. They would have performed all the ceremonies to prevent talk in the village. Or the people around would talk for generations of the sins committed by the family.

Kalyanikutty Edathi's children too would not have reached. It was now many years since Sankarana-rayanan, the eldest who had run away, died. Kalyanikutty Edathi did not know that. The second son was retarded. The third was Balagopalan. The family was only concerned that he should send money home every month. That would also stop once he was married. Only he had escaped the vicious circle. He had a job in the insurance company even if it was in a distant place.

'It isn't as though he sends lakhs. We won't miss the little he sends if he stops.' That was what the family said about the money Balagopalan sent every month. Kalyanikutty Edathi's children suffered from the handicap of having been born as her children.

'The son born of her womb has not come. What is the point of having all the ceremonies?' Raman Nair would have asked. The ceremonies were for the sake of the people around. The family must have felt grateful to Raman Nair for having said that.

'Kunhiraman from the next house has come on leave. They'll go back after a couple of weeks. When he goes, he'll put the bones in Haridwar or Rishikesh or some place like that.'

The Ganga flowed through Haridwar and Rishikesh. 'The Yamuna flows through Delhi', that was one of the children.

'How many times have I told you not talk when elders are discussing something. And not to hang around listening to older people either. Go in and study something.'

'No need for all that. Just put it in the Nila or some local river.' Nobody used the word immersion when discussing about Kalyanikutty Edathi's bones. No one was quite profane about it either.

No one even thought of building a platform for a tulasi somewhere in the yard. Kalyanikutty Edathi had never had any peace in her life. How would she then have eternal peace after life? They would console themselves with the thought, 'Kalyanikutty Edathi was not lucky enough to have all the ceremonies performed for her.' The family just waited for the fifteen days of the pula to be over.

The day after the minimal ceremonies were over Raman Nair had tea from the house. And sighed deeply. As though he was glad everything was over. Everything concerning Kalyanikutty Edathi was over as far as the family was concerned.

'A platform for tulasi', someone said.

'We'd decided there was no need for all that.'

'Even the place where Valiamma's

bones are kept is now overgrown and dirty. Who's to light the lamp every day and all that?' that was a female voice from inside.

Everything got over with her cremation. What a life! The people thought. Kalyanikutty Edathi had thought the same about herself when she lived. There would have been people in the family who grudged her the small piece of land where the pyre was lighted.

Finally the ashes were not immersed, not even thrown. They picked the bones as they were afraid of the people around. For a couple of days the bones were there under the tamarind tree in the southern compound. 'Some dog or the other will carry the bones away.' The implication was that not even animals would bother with those ashes and bones.

Four

Raman Nair would be of assistance in any venture. He was of great help to the people of the village. But he was also a great trouble to the people. Giving false evidence was something of a hobby with him. All of us knew that he had given evidence in a murder case and made the judge believe that the evidence produced by the police was false and that the accused had not actually committed the murder. Raman Nair's justification was that the accused had approached him first for help. He thought what he had done was only the right thing and did not see it as harm to the opposing group. Everyone around tried not to fall into his bad books. Three generations believed that the son born to Raman Nair in Padinjarath Ramani was now in the military and that he did not ever come to the village. No one paid much attention to those things. Raman Nair continued in his bachelor status.

'Anyway, it is only when important people die that there is all this fuss about picking the bones and immersing it and all that. So many poor people die in the village. Does anyone do all this for them? They are either buried or burnt and their story ends there,' Raman Nair continued his argument.

'Anyway, Christians and Muslims don't immerse ashes and bones in the Ganga and Perur to ensure salvation for their souls. Stop talking nonsense. I don't need to hear this.'

'Anyway, it wasn't as though she was very devout or something. She would go to the temple. But that was probably just to see someone,' Raman Nair added a dash of scandal to the conversation.

'And, Valiammama did not believe in all these rituals. He was a good Congressman,' that was another voice.

'Who's going to spend the money to go to Perur and Thirunavaya? Has her husband saved a lot of money for all this?'

No one said, 'I'll go.' If someone had come, new stories and scandals and accusations would have come out. And the person who came forward would have suffered for his interference.

Kalyanikutty Edathi's ashes received the same treatment that she had got when she was alive. Death did not bring a feeling of equality in anyone. They showed that she was unwanted even in their attitude towards the ashes.

Did anyone pray that another creature like this would not be born in the family? Kalyanikutty Edathi had never wondered why she had been cursed with a life like this. One had been born, may be one was fated to live such a life. 'Born as a human being in this sea of sorrow', she too used to chant the prayer that went like that. She had never felt that the next line which requested a helping hand to lift one from the sea of sorrows applied to her.

Five

Ammayi had given birth to Kalyanikutty Edathi one hour after sunset. It was dark by then. It was a Tuesday and the star was Pooradam.

'Why on earth did you have another daughter? You'll have to try again for a boy, won't you? I would like to die after seeing a boy born. You won't let me die in peace. One should have done good deeds in the past birth.' She had been yelled at because the child was a girl. Kalyanikutty Edathi entered this world listening to the curses of her own people. Her elder sister Saudamini was three years old by then. She had been pleased to have a younger sister at that time. Would the family have regretted that she was not a boy, she had wondered later. Anyway she escaped too much blame because she was the first one.

'Her seventh house is rather weak.

The moon is under a shadow as well. You may expect that she will have a late marriage.' Krishna Panikker had said when he cast her horoscope. All that was purely superstition. Instead of trying to bring up the child as well as she could be brought up, she was condemned to what was considered her fate from the beginning. Krishna Panikker's words provided the excuse that all the ill that her life held was due to the bad moment she had chosen to come into this life.

Nobody asked Krishna Panikker to write out Kalyanikutty Edathi's horoscope in full. When asked whether an elaborate horoscope should be written, it was Kumarettan who said that the plain chart would do. Nobody was interested in planets and their positions and their influence on this unwanted girl's life.

The next child was also a girl. People did mutter then too. 'Our fate, what else?' Krishna Panikker recommended, 'Send some offering to Sabarimala with someone who is going there. Light a lamp every evening at the Ayyappankavu here. The next will be a boy.'

'Your husband isn't all that old. He's healthy too. It isn't just rice that has gone into that body. He gets goat's liver from Beeran's shop every time he comes here to stay with you.' That was Muthassi who heard all this while she was reciting her prayers. She was also intoning, 'Narayana, Narayana' in between.

When she grew up, Kalyanikutty Edathi must have thought to herself that no one should be born as the second child. The first child born after a wait turned out to be a girl. They had wished for a boy. Still, the first child is always pampered in any family. The third one, though a girl again, was the last child in the family and thus petted for a long while. Kalyanikutty Edathi had often thought that it would have been better not to have been born at all rather than be born in the middle of these two. But what could she do?

The first was the first child and so valued, the third was the pampered last child. There was no point in her worrying about all that. She had often thought about Valiamma's second daughter, Rema, often compared her situation with her own. There wasn't much difference. But Rema would not bear as much as she would without protest. So she escaped the worst of it. Rema would burst into tears once in a while when it all got too much for her. She herself could not do that. What was the point in grumbling and complaining and making one's own life a misery. Bear it all, live through it, that was Kalyanikutty Edathi's principle.

Rema had once gone alone to the temple and had been yelled at by everyone. 'How dare you go alone? Who did you want to see at the temple that you can't go with someone else?' Grown up girls were never sent alone to the temple. There would be a whole lot of layabouts sitting in front of the temple just to look at the women who came. 'She has become very devout all of a sudden. From now on you'll only go if you can go with someone else.' But still, when compared with herself, Rema did have more freedom and consideration in her house.

When she was about twelve years old, Kalyanikutty Edathi's father had brought blouse pieces for his three daughters. Parameswarammaman didn't know anything about buying clothes and all that. He went to the textile shop, told them he wanted three pieces of cloth for stitching blouses, that cheap cotton would do, that they should all be similar. Even his wife ragged him about the patterns on the blouse pieces, ' He must have bought it from the coffee shop. The cloth is full of pictures of split coffee beans.'

There were three colours – blue, violet and green. Vanaja and Saudamini quickly grabbed the colours they liked. Kalyanikutty Edathi got the one that was left over. No one asked whether she liked it. Take what you get, eat whatever is there. That was the general attitude. Though the other two expressed their happiness at getting the new blouses, Kalyanikutty Edathi showed neither pleasure nor displeasure. Her attitude was, after all, I also got one, I wasn't omitted. She consoled herself with the thought that if her father had brought just two pieces, she would have got nothing. At least, he had thought of bringing three of them.

Saudaminiedathi and Vanaja got their blouses stitched immediately by tailor Kunhiraman. Vanaja had seen Kunhiraman go past the gate on his way to the toddy shop and had called him. She had a blouse to be given as a model ready in her hand. She also instructed him to lower the neckline in front. Kunhiraman laughed to himself. He had stitched the old blouse and was wondering what would happen if the neckline was lowered further in front. Saudaminiedathi also wanted it the same way. She also wanted the neckline at the back to be lower. She would have preferred to get it stitched without sleeves. But the people at home would raise a fuss. She consoled herself with the thought that they wouldn't notice if the neck was lower.

Kalyanikutty Edathi realised that her sisters had got their blouses stitched only when they went to the temple wearing the new blouses. They hadn't told her anything. She sent the blouse piece and an old blouse to Kunhiraman's tailoring shop. It was another week by the time she got the new blouse. She wore it to the temple that evening and had to hear the comment, 'She could hardly wait to wear the new blouse.' Her sleeves were shorter than those of her sister. 'Look at her, the sleeves are so short. She'll make them shorter and shorter till they just cover her shoulders, like the white women. Haven't you seen Kamala Nehru's photographs? The women in Ravi Varma pictures too wear short sleeves. But those are old pictures. She's showing off now.'

The next week they had to go for feast to celebrate their friend Sarojini's menarche. Saudamini Edathi and Vanaja told each other, 'It suits you.'

Kalyanikutty Edathi pretended she had not heard anything. She had learnt to pretend that she had not heard a lot of things. She felt better when she did not react to those comments. When she was in school, if she just tied her skirt a little higher, they would say even more, 'There comes the white madamma. After some time she will lift it as high as her knees. Maybe she'll shave her legs and paint her toes. Phoo!'

Six

Kalyanikutty Edathi did not curse anyone, not even her fate. She did not show any jealousy when her sisters were paid more attention, when they received more love and affection. She did not feel angry with those who loved her sisters more than herself. Kalyanikutty Edathi always behaved to her elder and younger sisters as a sister should, with affection. But they did not act as though they remembered that they had a sister like this. They were lucky, they enjoyed their luck. How could they be to blame for the fact that she did not get any affection? They too learnt to behave like this to her from the others in the house. What was the point in being jealous and grudging? A character who was denied the right to express her emotions. She had learnt early in life that she lived for the sake of others. She found peace of mind in that philosophy. It helped her retain her balance, her sanity. She had often felt that someone else in her place might have gone mad. Her attitude was that she was born to bear grief, to make sacrifices, to bear everything. At least that attitude saved trouble. This was a life meant to work for others, to suffer. She had felt that the people at home did not share even their griefs let alone their joys, with her. Listen to anything equably – that was the only way to live here. There wasn't a day when she did not wonder why she lived at all.

One could bear even disgrace. But why should anyone live, bearing the sarcasm and pointed comments of one's own people day in and day out. But such thoughts did not lead anywhere. Kalyanikutty Edathi faced life by covering her mind and intelligence so that they would not wake up.

Earlier Kalyanikutty Edathi used to wonder why even her parents had this attitude towards her. She did not find an answer to that question. After a while, she thought there was no point in burdening her mind with that worry as well and stopped thinking about it.

Though she was the second daughter, she too had been born of the same womb, her mother had had the same labour pains when she delivered her as well, hadn't she. One could understand her father's view point. He was hardly ever at home. When he did come home on holidays, he would just have time to speak to her mother about family matters. He would bring his children things. He never showed any partiality in what he brought for each of his daughters. Since he was not in the habit of petting them, there was no cause for complaint that he petted one of them more. Still, why did her father not realise the way the others in the family treated her! She was made to do all the work. If something special was to be made when her father visited, the rest would tell Kalyanikutty Edathi to do it. Though that was not a problem, he too would call her if he needed anything done.

There was one picture which would not fade from Kalyanikutty Edathi's mind. Whenever she saw the gooseberry tree on the eastern side of the house, she would remember that. It was Kalyanikutty Edathi who had planted that tree which bore fruit in abundance every year. But everyone had forgotten who planted it. They would say, 'It is wonderful to see that gooseberry tree with all the branches covered with fruit.' The fruits were given to the neighbouring houses in big bags. At home too, they would pickle the fruits in huge jars.

On one of his visits to the house, their father had made each of his daughters plant a tree on the eastern side of the house. The compound had trees on both the eastern and western side. These had been planted in the times of the great-uncle of whom people still talked. They were huge trees, with branches spreading out on all sides. There were trees planted by the later generations too. The locals would speak about the rich soil in that compound.

'You can't call it just soil. Gold grows there. Jack trees and mango trees yield fruit like they do nowhere else. Perhaps it is because they were planted by people who were lucky too.'

That time, when her father came he decided his daughters would also plant a tree each. Vanaja planted a jack tree, Saudamini a mango tree, and Kalyanikutty Edathi was asked to plant the gooseberry tree.

'The mango tree is the third year variety. You'll have fruits in three years. And jack tree is also the type which bears very sweet fruit.'

But the mango tree did not bear fruits in the third year. It took seven years to yield. Saudamini would look at the branches each year for the flowers. The jack tree too grew slowly.

There was a comment when Kalyanikutty Edathi planted the gooseberry sapling, 'It doesn't matter if that does not bear fruit. The tree in the northern compounds always has more fruits than needed.' The gooseberry that she planted too was cursed immediately. But no one noticed that that curse had not worked. When the tree started bearing fruits, they forgot the curse and even the fact that it was Kalyanikutty Edathi who had planted the tree.

The only person who had some sympathy for Kalyanikutty Edathi was her aunt. When she was very upset, when she could bear it no longer, she would go to Ammayi's house which wasn't very far off. Not that she could go whenever she felt like it. But, whenever she got the chance, she would rush to Ammayi. She would go and sit near her for a while. Ammayi would keep Kalyanikutty Edathi's hand in hers for a while.

Ammayi felt, 'Poor girl!' But she did not say that. Ammayi knew the kind of problems Kalyanikutty was facing. She knew that the family made Kalyanikutty do all the work in the house and that no one ever lent a hand. And that whatever she did, she would only be criticised. Ammayi had also said to herself, 'What a life!'

Kalyanikutty Edathi had often wondered why only Ammayi had this soft corner for her. When she came to this family as the wife of Kalyanikutty Edathi's uncle, Ammayi too must have felt an outsider. Perhaps she too was made to do all the work. It would only be after they moved into a house of their own that Ammayi would have been able to lead a normal life. She would not have forgotten those stories. It would be those memories which made Ammayi show such sympathy, Kalyanikutty Edathi thought.

On days when she went to Ammayi's house, there would be comments at home.

'She's gone visiting today.'

'That woman wants to know what is happening here.'

'Kalyanikutty must be adding

plenty of colour to all the stories.'

'She would enjoy listening to those stories too.'

'It isn't that she likes Kalyanikutty particularly. Just wants to listen to gossip.'

'Or why does she give her sweets and things every visit.'

'I believe she gives her tea and sweets each time she goes there.'

'Kalyanikutty must be going there for that.'

'As if she doesn't get enough to eat here.'

When she got back home, she would have to face the sarcastic comments and knowing smiles of the family.

'She's come back after the feast.'

'You've had your fill, haven't you?'

'She must have filled that woman's stomach with stories.'

'Why do you keep going there, anyway?'

There would be comments about Kalyanikutty Edathi going to the temple as well.

'There isn't any point in going to the temple to pray for luck. One has to be born at the right time.'

Kalyanikutty Edathi had observed the Monday fast which young women observe to get a good husband.

'Even a thousand fasts and penances are not going to be enough. Who does she think she'll get? A bridegroom from the royal family or something?'

There was another friend whom Kalyanikutty Edathi always thought of with affection. That was Narayani Cheriyamma's daughter Vesamani. She'd always had admiration for Vesamani, never any envy. She was born lucky, Kalyanikutty Edathi thought, but did not grumble that she herself had never had any luck.

Vesamani was fairly good-looking. Though she was a little on the plump side, she was sufficiently tall for that not to show. She was always bright. Not that she got any special privilege as Narayani Cheriamma's only daughter. She too had to do all the work in her house. She too had been allowed to study only till the tenth standard. But her parents never scolded her or cursed her. Vesamani too never had any complaints about anyone.

It was when Vesamani reached her eighteenth year that the Postmaster Krishnan Nair brought that proposal. Krishnan Nair had got acquainted with Nilakantan Namboodiri of Kalloopara illam when he had been postmaster at Kalloopara.

Nilakantan Namboodiri always reached the Post Office in time to see the mailbag arrive. He would stand and watch when the postal peon Kochunni opened the sack and put the postal seal on the letters that came. He would watch with bated breath when Kochunni picked up the leather bag in which the Money Orders came and gave it to the Postmaster, and the Postmaster opened it with the key he had, took out the money and counted it, handing it over with the forms to the postman to be given to the addressees. He found it fascinating that the money which came from such distances reached the person it was meant for with such accuracy.

Nilakantan Namboodiri had often dreamt of someone sending him such a Money Order. When the postman Kochunni brought it, he would sign for it and take the money. The picture was very clear in his mind. He had a relative in Madras. He could ask that chap to send him a money order of fifty rupees. He certainly would. But when the money order reached the illam his father would raise cain. 'Where is it from? Who sent it? Why did he sent it?' the questions would be endless. But to go to the post office and collect it would not be dignified.

'Imagine sending money to the

illam! Who thought of this stupid thing? Insulting the whole family!' Nilakantan Namboodiri could imagine what his father would say. And if he realised that his son was behind it, he would get some punishment which would just about fall short of complete ostracism.

Another dream that Nilakantan Namboodiri had was to sit behind the ticket counter in a railway station. You gave the money to the man behind the window, a piece of cardboard was pushed into a machine and once you got it you could travel by train. He wished he could sit behind that window. On the northern side of the illam, away from the eyes of his father who sat in the front verandah, he would sit at a window and start selling tickets. He would call out to the children who passed that way to play and say, 'Come, come. Don't you want tickets? Come and buy some.' Two boys came by one day. Instead of buying tickets, they said, 'This isn't any ticket, he's just tricking everyone.' Nilakantan Namboodiri got really mad. But he didn't know any swear words to yell at the children. So he called them, 'Snake gourd! Pumpkin!'

One day, the woodcutter's son Chinnan came in and asked, 'A ticket please.'

'Hai, hai, you've gone and polluted the place,' and the counter was closed for ever.

Postmaster Krishnan Nair whispered in Nilakantan Namboodiri's ear, 'Thirumeni, isn't it time you got a wife?'

'What are you saying Krishnan? Don't joke about such things.'

'It wasn't a joke. Everything that is to be done should be done in its proper time.'

'What do you mean by everything that is to be done?' Nilakantan Namboodiri was shaking with laughter when he asked that.

'You are only the third in line, aren't you. By the time you are the eldest and marry from your own caste you will be quite old. I just thought, what is the point in getting married when you are old?'

'So. Though you're a fool quite often, once in a while you get intelligent too, do you? All right. Have you thought of anyone?

'Yes, I have.'

'Have you seen the girl? You do know that I'm not getting married to support the girl's family, don't you?'

'They'll be pleased to welcome you as a bridegroom. And she'll suit you. She's good looking, very fair. If you'll just consider it...'

'Why not? But who'll bell the cat? That is, tell my father?'

'When it's only this sort of agreement, you just need permission from the girl's people. It's not as though it is a proper marriage and you need to take the girl to your illam.'

'That's true. How far is it?'

'You can set out from here in the afternoon and reach there before dusk.'

'I see. That's good. I'll reach there at the correct time, what?' Thirumeni laughed once more.

Nilakantan Namboodiri would go to Vesamani's house only three or four times in a month. Before this morganatic alliance had been fixed, Karunakaran Nair, Vesamani's uncle had said, 'It won't be possible to arrange for a brahmin cook to prepare food for the Namboodiri here. There aren't any cooks like that available hereabouts.'

Krishnan Nair had informed Nilakantan Namboodiri of this.

'That's all right. I'll eat upma or some such thing. That will do. Just don't let the people at my illam know that I'm eating stuff not cooked by brahmins.'

When Nilakantan Namboodiri came on his visits, he wanted Vesamani beside him all the time. He wouldn't stir out of the room and he would not let her go away either. Not even go to the veranda.

'Let the others look after everything today. Don't go anywhere, Vesa.'

The rest of the family also did not say anything. After all, the Namboodiri came only a couple of times in a month.

He would talk of the time when he would be the eldest in the family and would have to marry within his own caste, 'I'll be old by then. What is the point in getting married then? Vesa'll do for me.'

When Nilakantan Namboodiri came on his visits, Vesamani would not even go to the temple.

'The god in the temple will still be there. I can only stay for two days.' Tirumeni would object if Vesamani started out to the temple. And so she didn't go anywhere on days when he was at home.

Normally, when she went to the temple she would meet Kalyanikutty Edathi. If they both had time, they would exchange a few words with each other. Vesamani always appeared happy when they met after a visit from the Tirumeni. She did not seem to mind that her so-called husband could not be with her all the time. She probably felt that marrying someone from her own caste and having to take care of all his comforts and needs would have been more of a bother than this casual arrangement. Tirumeni adored her. He seemed to be sure that he didn't need to marry a woman of his own caste. He had never been angry with her or rude to her. He appeared to think of Vesamani as a rare toy which had come into his possession. Vesamani did not try to take advantage of his craze for her either.

Kalyanikutty Edathi had watched this relationship between Vesamani and her Namboodiri with interest. But she was sure that not many were destined to enjoy such a relationship and so did not even wish that she, Kalyanikutty, would get a man like that. She prayed every day that Vesamani would continue to be happy.

Muthassi would get up early in the morning. She would sit on the southern verandah and recite her prayers. As she recited, she would cut the vegetables for the curries to be made that day, in different lengths and thicknesses. Along with the prayers, she would be calling to Kalyanikutty Edathi as well.

'Get everything ready early. See that the rice is not overcooked as it was yesterday.'

'See that the iddlies don't turn out like stones.'

'Don't put too much salt in the curry.'

'The coconut should be ground

finely.' The instructions would continue incessantly. All these were addressed to Kalyanikutty Edathi. She would keep Vanaja and Saudamini by her and talk to them of other things.

'Heat up some sesame oil with pepper in it for Saudamini. Heat it properly and then cool it. Her hair is falling terribly.'

Everyone was bothered about Vanaja and Saudamini. Kalyanikutty Edathi also had to work so that their lives were comfortable. All of them forgot that she was also one of the sisters. Even the servants took their tone from the members of the family. If she told the maid to wash some dishes immediately, pat would come the reply, 'Let me just finish sweeping here.' Since she needed the vessels urgently, Kalyanikutty Edathi would wash them herself. Of if she instructed the servant, 'Hang out these washed clothes now. The sun has come out.' The maid would vanish with an 'In a moment' and Kalyanikutty Edathi would have to do not just the washing, but the hanging out and the folding up as well.

The local people often discussed her fate.

'Kalyanikutty does all the work in that house.'

'Like a maidservant.'

'The other two females dress themselves up and sit around decoratively.'

'Can't her parents do something?'

'That grandmother of theirs is there, isn't she?'

'Poor thing.'

Kalyanikutty Edathi got the certificate 'poor thing' from everyone. But she did not get affection or sympathy from anywhere.

She did not wonder why she was born. Since she was born she had to live here somehow, she had to learn to do so. She had often wondered if every second child faced the same problems. This thought came when she thought of Kunhilaksmiedathi's daughter Parvathi. But she was slightly better off.

Kunhilakshmiedathi was Kalyanikutty Edathi's aunt's daughter. Parvathi and Kalyanikutty Edathi used to go to school together. She used to confide all sorts of painful things to her those days. She could not speak of those things to anyone else. They would only yell if they heard her complaints.

Kalyanikutty Edathi would go in the morning on her way to the school to Parvathi's house and call out to her from the gate. By the time Parvathi replied someone would have yelled out, 'Aren't you going to school today? That girl's been calling out to you for ages. If you do plan to go today come out fast.'

'It isn't as though she is going to learn and become somone,' would be the comment. They planned to get her married off long before she passed any exams.

Kalyanikutty Edathi was good at her studies. Saudamini Edathi and Vanaja needed tuitions to get through their classes. In spite of private coaching they did not get as good marks as Kalyanikutty Edathi did. But no one bothered to comment on that. She consoled herself with the thought that at least people did not say that she had got the marks by cheating. No one said, 'Good!' or 'Bright Girl!'. She knew that there was no point in dreaming of a college education. Her sisters were only interested in getting through the high school somehow. Saudamini Edathi stopped studying after the seventh. Vanaja failed in the tenth.

Kumarettan did not like to see Kalyanikutty Edathi go to school. Wearing a long skirt and blouse, with her waist-length hair combed with a small plait in the middle, she looked good. Her long lashes and the short hair falling over her forehead made her eyes look bright.

She was well-shaped for her age. His fear was that people were watching her. 'Bitch', he muttered to himself. Kumarettan too had a hand in stopping her studies. 'It's time we got her married to someone.' Her uncle's son had finished studying. He was employed at Bangalore. Even if the horoscopes matched, there was no guarantee that he would be willing to marry her. It would be better to find someone from outside to marry her and take her away from here.

'Bhargavi and Nanikutty are the same age as Kalyanikutty. Her friends too. If they have all stopped studying, what is the point in sending her all decked up every day?' That was Muthassi. She had hoped that Muthassi would have some sympathy for her. She had gone over to the other side too. The nearest college was about sixteen miles away from the house. She could stay there with the family of one of Kumarettan's friends. But there was only a mother and four young sons staying there. How could they send her there with the confidence that there would be no scandal? To go daily from the house to the college was not practical. Everyone agreed with Muthassi. Her dream of growing up to stand on her own feet collapsed like that. There was no point in carrying that dream of an education in her mind. She could break those castles she had built in her mind. There was no place for determination and courage either. They would also be driven away as in the ceremonial casting out of the evil goddess at end of the month of Mithunam.

On the rare occasions when she got time, Kalyanikutty Edathi would sit outside on the back veranda or in the hall next to it and read. She would get magazines and weeklies from the next house once in a while. 'Look at that. One would think she is preparing for some examination. She has no thought about what is kept on the fire. Milk would have boiled over and got burnt.' But in spite of the comments, she found some faint relief from her drudgery in that world of letters.

She thought she'd been lucky she'd been allowed to study upto the tenth standard. Her mistake had been in dreaming of a college life. If she sat somewhere thinking about all this in her rare moments of leisure, they would ask, 'Who are you dreaming of in this broad daylight?'

Once she finished school, Kalyanikutty Edathi had more and more housework to do. There was someone to sweep the yard and wash the dishes. But Kalyanikutty Edathi had to make the lunch and tea and the rest of it. Even Matha who came to sweep and wash dishes did not have so much work to do. And she was paid for the work she did. Kalyanikutty Edathi did not get paid and also did not get even a word of appreciation from anyone. She had to get up early in the morning and make tea for everyone. The others in the family would get up only by the time she'd blown the fire in the hearth to life and made tea. Muthassi would have started reciting her prayers. In the middle of it, she would also say what was to be made for lunch. Saudamini Edathi and Vanaja would get up only after everything was ready.

'Kalyani, ask that boy to pluck some mangoes from the tree and make a good perukku. Vanaja likes it a lot. We'll have kanji and a curry made with greengram. Don't put too much coconut in the curry.' All Muthassi's instructions were addressed to Kalyanikutty Edathi. She would do everything. And the rest of the family would wait for the dishes to appear, in the confident expectation that she would have made everything.

One afternoon someone found a hair in the rice. 'Must be hers.' The verdict was immediate. There were other women in the house. Others worked in the kitchen. If there were stones in the rice, Kumarettan would find them. He was the one who found the hair too. One day, he got up with his lunch half-eaten because he bit on a small stone in the rice. 'This is what happens if you don't search through the rice properly.' The accusation was addressed to Kalyanikutty Edathi.

'What does it matter if she loses some hair. As long as she doesn't leave the hair around in our food. She'll grow bald soon if she loses hair like this.' The comment was not one of sympathy.

Kalyanikutty Edathi had lots of hair. The other two sisters used specially prepared oil to make their hair grow. Kalyanikutty Edathi rarely had time to have a leisurely bath or to use thali on her hair or even comb her hair and let it dry. She had to attend to so many people's needs. She did not say, 'I don't get any peace.' There was no one to listen to her or to take the complaint seriously.

'She says she has a headache.'

'Must be her breasts growing.' She'd heard Muthassi say that.

All Kalyanikutty Edathi's requests and needs were rejected right from the time she was a child.

Kalyanikutty Edathi liked teaching the children in the evening and reciting verses to them. She'd finish the cooking for the night as quickly as possible and then call the children at dusk. And she would teach them the verses that all children normally recite at that time. And then make them repeat the multiplication tables from one to sixteen. You had to reach 'sixteen sixteens are two hundred and fifty six' before you could stop. After a few days, she would teach them verses from Srikrishnacharitam manipravalam and some of the poems of poets like Asan and Vallathol Srikrishna-charitam would be learnt, starting from the twelfth chapter.

That chapter had to be memorised within one week. It was only later that the children realised that this exercise was very good for developing memory. At that time, mostly they grumbled about this enforced learning.

Seven

'Kalyanikutty's grown up', it was Muthassi who made the declaration. 'She can't rush around with boys any more. She has to behave, be quiet and modest.' No one would say that Kalyanikutty Edathi was not quiet and modest. Muthassi was just announcing the rules of behaviour that were to be followed under the circumstances.

Kalyanikutty Edathi found this a new cross to bear. Even otherwise she did not feel a part of the family. Now at these times it was worse. But there was one consolation where this was concerned. There was no discrimination shown here. Everyone knew which female in the family was having her periods.

The menses taboos were strictly observed for those six or seven days. Kalyanikutty Edathi felt that she was treated more harshly than the others even where these taboos were concerned. But her feelings were not allowed to become concrete thoughts and express themselves. Kalyanikutty Edathi showed an unusual tolerance where such things were concerned. One wondered from where she got this tolerance. Nobody else in the family had it. When people behaved extremely badly to her, her mother would sometimes feel bad. Kalyanikutty Edathi's father did not pay much attention to what went on in the household. Kalyanikutty Edathi's eyes never overflowed with tears. She must have carried them in her heart. Or perhaps, her tears must have dried up.

On those days of taboo, Kalyanikutty Edathi would get her food only after the rest of the family had had theirs. Sometimes it would be only when Kareem got fed. Kareem was the trusty canine of the family. When she had her periods, food would be served in a separate plate and glass set aside for the purpose. Since it was believed that the person who served the food would also be polluted if a second helping was served, they would put a lot of rice the first time. On top of that a lot of curry would be poured. If there was anything left over, the woman concerned had to throw it under some plantain tree or the other and wash the plate and leave it bottom up on the verandah. Even Kareem's plate was washed by the maid. Kalyanikutty Edathi had prayed that such days of untouchability should not be visited on any woman. A separate mat and pillow were provided for the use of the polluted woman on those days. After the days of menses were over, these had to be dipped into the pond. It was a sort of echo of the behaviour that people of lower castes had to face in those days. She would think of the fact that Nairs behaved like that to the lower castes all the time. Such a lack of humanity in their behaviour.

Kalyanikutty Edathi's menarche was not celebrated as was usual. She did not go with her friends to the pond outside for the ceremonial bath.

Saudamini Edathi had gone with six friends for the bath. The friends had ragged Saudamini Edathi. The girls who attained puberty went to the outside pond and bathed there ceremonially with their friends to make an announcement to the world. The bath and celebrations meant 'Here is a girl prepared for marriage.' Where Kalyanikutty Edathi was concerned even that announcement was not made. It will all be according to her fate. Let her fate be decided by the lines on her head. Kalyanikutty Edathi too did not blame anyone. She too thought that her fate would take its course.

She wore a new skirt and blouse to the temple the day after the ritual bath at the end of the periods.

'Why are you all decked up today? So, you didn't call us for the function?' her friends asked. Kalyanikutty Edathi did not reply.

'You think no one will know about all this if you don't invite us. Just wait and see, we'll tell everyone at school.'

The other girls made Kalyanikutty Edathi sit at the very end of a bench that day. The next girl sat a little away from her. When the master came to the classroom he noticed the way the girls were sitting, but did not comment on it. He did not ask about it either. The other girls laughed among themselves. That was how the declaration of maturity was made in Kalyanikutty Edathi's case.

'You have to sit apart for four days in a month from now on. We have to have a bath as soon as we get home. They won't give us anything otherwise.'

'A full four days.'

'You can't fold your hands to the deity when you pass the temple.' They instructed her on the modes of behaviour.

Kalyanikutty Edathi wanted to ask if she could not pray in her mind at least, but she did not ask them that. She did not ask anyone to clear that doubt. Since no one, not even god, heard her prayers anyway, she continued to pray in her mind.

She could not go near the lamp when it was lighted at dusk, nor near the children who recited their prayers, in case they were polluted.

She did believe in God. And used to go to the temple every morning. It was usually she who lighted the lamp at dusk and placed it in front of the house. No one had ever said that she was an unbeliever. Once in a while she had wondered why she did all this, what purpose it served. One could say she prayed more for the sake of others in the family than for herself. Her peace of mind and contentment depended so much on the state of mind of the others. She could have peace only if her prayer 'God, please show them the right path' was answered. She only wanted to live like a human being. All her prayers were for that. Though she did not feel her prayers were being answered, she did not stop praying.

Kalyanikutty Edathi often thought about those who were unable to take birth as the first child or the last. It was mostly such children who did not get any sort of affection or peace in the family. Whether the child was a boy or a girl, there was no difference in the way the family behaved to them.

When she had been a small child, this had been the attitude of the elders to her. When Vanaja, her younger sister, had been a child, everyone had been so fond of her! She could remember the fuss they used to make of Saudamini who was three years older than her. Once in a while she would compare those attitudes to the one everyone displayed to her. It wasn't that she suffered from a feeling of inferiority or anything of that sort. There was a very marked difference in the behaviour of the family towards her and her sisters.

'Today is Kalyanikutty's birthday.'

So make payasam. On the other girls' birthdays there would be special offerings at the temple and special preparations at home. 'It isn't as though she was born on a special day. Her fate will be what it is.'

Once, when a distant relative came from Bombay, he'd brought slabs of chocolate. After it had been divided up among all the rest, Kalyanikutty had got a small piece. At the end of it someone had called out, 'Kalyanikutty!'. It was as though the very call said you can have it if you want.

Kalyanikutty Edathi always wished for silence. She would not answer anyone unless absolutely necessary. She never explained either. If she gave an answer, it would be interpreted as cheek. So whatever anyone asked, she would reply in a couple of words, and if possible, in one.

'I asked that dumb creature.'

'She's deaf. You have to ask her at least three times before you get an answer.'

Kalyanikutty Edathi pretended that she did not hear those remarks. She felt that her attitude was the safest in her circumstances.

Vadakkotte Ramanarayanan, Gouridasan and Padmakumaran had been born in alternate years. Gouridasan was never treated as Ramanarayanan and Padmakumaran were. They treated him like those bull calves which are given to the temples. The family's attention was focused on the eldest and the youngest. Gouridasan continued in the village. He joined the Congress. After a while, his wandering in the village earned him the qualification to become a Panchayat member. Gouridasan had claimed even earlier that the panchayat member was also entitled to speak at meetings when M.P.s and ministers came to the village. But when the President came to the Panchayat, he was denied the opportunity. His party claimed that it was due to paucity of time. Gouridasan stood for election as the candidate of the Communist party in the next election and lost. He made plans to join the Congress again. He went to Thiruvananthapuram with some MLAs with some petitions. He wrote letters to the ministers about what he felt had to be done. Finally, he became a teacher in a private school there. He had decided that he would become the Secretary of the Private School Teachers' Association and teach the Party a lesson using the Association. Nothing worked. His main occupations were reading the newspaper and interfering in anything that happened in the village. The family had paid more attention to the education of the other two. They appeared to feel that it did not matter even if the second one went astray. When Ramanarayanan wrote his examinations, the lamp in the puja room would be kept alight the whole time. The day after the examinations there would be special pujas and offerings in the Devi temple nearby. When Gouridasan went to the school to write his examinations, no one would even call out, 'Go to the puja room and pray before the deities.' What they were likely to say was, 'If you study, you will pass. But where does he have the time for all that? He spends all his time playing. Let's hope he does not score zero in the exams.' When Gouridasan scored more than sixty percent they must have suspected that the master who corrected the papers made a mistake. No one even thought of sending him for higher studies.

'He can try for a job in Coimbatore Municipality. They need people there. That Sekharan Nair who has a job in the bus company has some hold there. We'll tell him to try.'

But it was not Gouridasan's, but Kavilangate Meenakshi's story that consoled Kalyanikutty Edathi. Venugopalan was the eldest there. Meenakshi had only two brothers, one elder to her and one younger than her. But she did not get even a fraction of the affection and pampering that the two boys got. When Venugopalan was young, hardly anybody called him by his name. It was all pet and love and sweetie and so on. Then those pet names went into disuse. They came out again when the younger boy was born. When Meenakshi was born those words were never used. They might have just forgotten to use them. Though she was the only daughter, she did not get any privileges because of that.

Once when she thought about it, Kalyanikutty Edathi thought that the Government was right. No one should have more than two children. If so, both the children would get consideration and affection. That was what made a family contented. The ones who got born in between were like weeds.

Venugopalan failed twice in the tenth standard. He wanted to join the army. 'You need the minimum height for that,' Gopalan who studied with Venugopalan said.

'You don't need to be tall to fight wars. What nonsense!' Venugopalan's mother commented. 'Wasn't Napoleon a short man?'

'Yes, but he was the General. He's speaking of joining in the army as an ordinary soldier.' Everyone was surprised that Gopalan could speak about Napoleon and his height.

'Book learning isn't everything, do you understand?' Gopalan retorted.

Venugopalan did not feel that he had lost the opportunity to serve his country just because he lacked height.

Meenakshi's life was also like Kalyanikutty Edathi's. But she was not as submissive. If someone yelled at her, she would yell right back.

'She's very impertinent,' if someone said so they would be told to shut their ears if they didn't want to hear what she said.

'She's getting above herself.'

'I've more to give you.'

'Who gave birth to this creature?'

'Don't you know?'

'Stop being cheeky!'

Gopalan had given great publicity to the question about who gave birth to the creature, and don't you know. Gopalan was good at telling stories.

Gopalan's new tales always circulated fast and lasted for a while.

Her family decided that Meenakshi had to be married off as soon as possible. 'We can't keep her in this shed for long. We have to send her off to some other cowshed,' her uncle said.

Eight

The man who came to marry Meenakshi was short, fat and dark. His name was Raghavan.

'He looks like a toddy tapper.'

'Not so loudly.'

'He doesn't want any dowry, they say.'

'That must be why they are marrying her off to that peculiar looking creature.'

Even if they did ask for a dowry, it would be a small one. Anyway, Meenakshi would be lucky to get a bridegroom at all.

Meenakshi wished to move to new surroundings. Her husband's place was just two miles away. Meenakshi liked the new atmosphere. There was no one there to yell at her or curse her or find fault with her. He was not someone she had sought out. He was a partner found for her by her family, though they weren't really interested in getting someone good. Raghavan became the companion who gave her solace.

Kalyanikutty Edathi did not know whom her family would find for her. There was no point in dreaming about it or even thinking about it. So she did not waste time on daydreams. Housework did not permit her to spend time on daydreams either.

Saudamini's daughter wanted to learn classical dancing. Her dance teacher was Natanamandalam Gopinath who had graduated from Chembai Sangita Vidyalaya. He had even sung before Chembai Vaidyanatha Bhagavatar himself. He had once had to go to Delhi to receive the second prize awarded in All India Radio's Carnatic Classical music competition. He earned his living by the occasional concerts he got and teaching music. He had refused to get married in spite of his mother Alamelu Ammal's best persuasions. It was later that he had got obsessed with dance. The fame and the glory that stage stalwarts like Guru Kunchu Kurup earned attracted Gopi towards dance. He had been to cities like Bombay, Madras and Delhi with various dance troupes. Though professional dance troupes were rather wary of taking Gopi along with them when there were young female performers. Gopi was equally crazy about dance and the company of young women. Anyway, he realised that there was more income to be had from dance than from music.

Giving the dance master tea as soon as he came was another duty allotted to Kalyanikutty Edathi. Gopi would not take the cup in his hand, it had to be placed before him. He would come to the house at about four in the evening, hang the umbrella with its curved handle on the ring on the veranda wall and sit on the bench. By the time Saudamini sent her daughter, he would be ready to teach. When everyone else in the family was having their tea, Kalyanikutty Edathi would take Gopi his tea. Gopi was not bad-looking. He was very smart. He needed to smoke a cigarette after his tea. But as it was not possible to smoke in the house, Gopi would smoke his cigarette as soon as he went out of the gatehouse and into the lane.

'Gopi has curly hair.'

'He doesn't need a comb for his hair, it falls naturally,' Gopalan.

'The hair style suits the long face. Good that he does not have a moustache.'

'How did he get this curly hair and beetlebrows?'

'I'll tell you all that later,' Gopalan had not had a chance to cook up a story.

'You haven't thought up a story yet, have you?'

'It's not that. You won't understand if I tell you now. I'll tell you later when we have more time.' Gopalan escaped with that. He did not let them extend the stories and the questions.

When he went to Barber Velayudhan to get his hair cut, Gopi would say, 'Clean up my eyebrows as well, will you?' Velayudhan would trim the hair that curled up into his forehead from his eyebrows. When he put on the spectacles and looked into the mirror, his face would show his happiness. When Gopi came for the dance class, Kareem would not bark. But when he started actually teaching, he would put on his specs and then Kareem would start barking as well. When he put on his specs, the Bhagavatar's face took on an expression of cruelty. At first, Kareem was a big problem. Slowly, the dog got to know the dance master with his specs.

Kalyanikutty Edathi started talking to Gopi when she took him his tea. Gopi started it. He would tell her some news, ask her about things in the village. Sometimes, a story or a poem which appeared in the weekly would be the topic. The family started thinking that the conversations between the two were lengthening rather unnecessarily. Gopi and Kalyanikutty Edathi did not notice that their conversatins were getting longer. They did not feel that others were getting suspicious either. Earlier, he was not very regular with the classes. Nowadays, he always came on time, and would linger for a while after the classes. The people around started wondering if Gopi had another interest in coming to the house besides teaching the young girl classical dance. But the doubts became stronger when they observed the changes that occurred in Kalyanikutty Edathi. She never used to open her mouth except when forced to. She had now started humming a few lines from some poems. One day, as she hung out the clothes, she was heard reciting verses from Ramanan, the quintessential love poem. Kalyanikutty Edathi was the only person in the house who had read the Malayalam books and the Malayalam translations of Kalidasa's works lying around at home.

She had even read Nalappadan's Ratisamrajyam. It was Kalyanikutty Edathi who taught Saudamini Edathi's children some prayers and verses from poems. No one had objected to that then. When Ammaman came home, everyone would eat early and sit around to play a game of verses. The game went around with each person picking up the first letter of the third line and reciting in his turn a verse which started with that letter. Kalyanikutty Edathi did not usually have time to join in. She would be washing vessels or cleaning the kitchen or something at that time. If someone failed to find a verse in his turn it was Muthassi who usually came to the rescue. If Muthassi also failed, she would ask the children to ask Kalyanikutty Edathi. She would come and give the right verse and then vanish into the kitchen.

One day there was a muttered discussion in the house. As usual, the topic was Kalyanikutty Edathi. It went on under people's breath so that Kalyanikutty Edathi would not hear.

'The cheek of the guy!'

'How dare he?'

'Why blame him? She's the one who goes and stays chatting.'

'We don't know if he's a brahmin or a nair.'

'I didn't like the look of him when he started coming here. Didn't seem quite all right.'

'As long as he doesn't get anyone into trouble.

'He probably has someone in every place he goes to.'

The imagination of the accusatory group was going wild. The proposition was presented. The subject was Kalyanikutty Edathi. There was no voice heard against the proposition. The decision was unanimous. If the decision was heard outside, it would spread all over the village. No one thought of all that.

'He goes to the temple at exactly the same time she does.'

'They must be meeting each other in the lane.'

'Wonder what they plan to do?'

'They say nothing can stop a determined woman.'

'It is the silent cat that breaks the pot.'

If this reaches the ears of Gopalan or someone like that, the whole village will be ringing with scandal.

One afternoon, when lunch was over, Kalyanikutty Edathi was brought to the family conclave as an accused. The verdict was already decided on, it was only a matter of declaring it. There was no trial, no evidence, no examination of witnesses. Even the accusation was not spelt out. That was how the family court functioned. The verdict would be given with the unquestioned power of a king's verdict.

'You are becoming more and more impudent.'

'If uncle comes to know of this, he'll throw you out of the house.'

There was only the threat of punishment. The sentence had been stayed for the while.

Kalyanikutty Edathi had not travelled as far as the family had, in thinking about Gopi. She could ask the family court if the guilt was that she had at long last found someone who thought of her as another human being and spoke to her on those terms. But she knew that if she raised any question, the sentence would come into force immediately. That was what the rest of the family was like.

'If you have any such idea in mind, you'd better forget it. Be very careful.'

'Only Nairs from very good families, or members of the royal households, or Namboodiris from famous illoms have married into this family.'

'Do you think we'll permit a dance master to enter the family and disgrace it?'

'Don't attempt to blacken the name of the tharavad.'

'Imagine having to give food to a dancer along with the men who've married your sisters. They'll divorce their wives.'

Kalyanikutty Edathi stood silent before the accusers. They were all wondering how much harm would be done to the family's name by the relationship between Kalyanikutty Edathi and Gopi. There was no point in saying that there was no such relationship, their minds would refuse to accept that. The only escape was to stand there silently.

Gopi was not aware of all this. The usual tea was not forbidden. They did not stop the dance class abruptly either, in case people asked why. But Gopi could feel that there was something different in the behaviour of the family. Nothing was as it was before. Saudamini Edathi told Gopi one day, ' Bina has a lot to study at school. She's finding it difficult to manage her studies and dance and everything.' He wondered if it was a sort of foreword to saying that she need not learn dance.

One day, Kalyanikutty Edathi came and kept the cup of tea before Gopi and went away without a word. Gopi did not even see the expression on her face.

'Whore,' Gopi too heard someone saying that inside. It was the invective Kalyanikutty Edathi had earned by breaking a prohibition. She'd made the tea and it was growing cold since no one took it to the dance master. That was why she had taken it herself. Still, no one had ever called her a name like this.

'She has no sense of shame. She'll flirt with anyone.'

No one had ever insulted her like this before. She had heard that Thodikkal Paru was a whore, that men came and went in her house at odd times.

'That woman brought a bad name to the whole village. Now this one will bring a bad name to the tharavad.'

The topic of discussion was how Kalyanikutty Edathi dared do such things. Kalyanikutty Edathi knew that muttering about her behaviour was on the rise and that she was becoming more and more isolated. The secretive quality of the discussions were also being lost. Opinions were now being expressed in the servants' hearing. The mutters had now become open comments and sarcastic laughter.

That word 'whore' kept echoing in Kalyanikutty Edathi's ears. Who would recognize her grief at being thought such a low creature by everyone in the family? Let her grief become illness, she kept it in her heart and went on with her routine. She felt as though the very walls yelled out 'whore, whore' at her. As though someone woke her up at night calling her that. As though the word echoed in the well as she drew up water.

No one knew how helpless Kalyanikutty Edathi felt. She did not hold any grudge against anyone. She did not even ask herself whether there would ever be anyone to understand her, to sympathise with her. She just grieved that fate held only such experiences for her.

Gopi gave up teaching dance and went to Bombay with a distant relative. Kalyanikutty Edathi found out about it only later. She did not feel any disappointment that he no longer came. She prayed that he would not feel that he had to go away because of her. And consoled herself with the thought that no one would be able to yell at her about this again. The echo of the word 'whore' lingered within the four walls of the house as far as she was concerned. One could say the word took up permanent residence there. She felt as though she could hear that word from all sides. She knew that the life of the dancer which had hardly started, ended its contact with hers at this point. This became just one experience which they passed through.

Kittunni Nair had also heard the conversations going on in the house about Kalyanikutty Edathi. He did not enquire further into the matter. He was afraid that if he enquired too closely, he would be asked to get out of the house. Kittunni Nair was the karyasthan there, he managed the day to day affairs of property.

Kittunni Nair saw all the women in the village with the same eye. Gopalan's description was, 'Nair in search of an opportunity'. Wonder who she is, wonder where she is from, wonder if I can get her, so went his thought process. But he would choose his time and place to approach the woman. Once in a while he would pass the huge pond attached to the Namboodiri mana in the evening when the women bathed there. He would wait for Malu in the lane as she went home from work. His philosophy was that one had to keep casting baits and the fish would land one day.

Kittunni Nair had also heard that

there was something going on between dance master Gopi and Kalyanikutty Edathi. Once in a while one of the family, while yelling at Kalyanikutty Edathi would say, 'Now that Kittunni Nair will also come in search of you'. Since he had followed all this, he felt that he would not be blamed too much if he too tried a hand. They would only tell Kalyanikutty Edathi, 'Don't you know what he is like? Why weren't you more careful?'

Gopalan says that Kittunni Nair has netted many of the women who worked in the houses in the village. But he was very particular about religion and caste. He would try to seduce only Nair women. He had decided to make an exception in Malu's case alone. Malu was very fair, much fairer than him. Kittunni Nair did not hold a grudge against the woman if she eluded him. He did not grieve over such losses either. 'Her loss' was the only thought that came to his mind on such occasions. But he did not necessarily withdraw because of one rejection.

When he heard all the talk about

Kalyanikutty Edathi, Kittunni Nair had a desire, 'Why not make a try?'

One afternoon, Kittunni Nair set out on his mission. He came and stood in the yard before the verandah and started making conversation. Kalyanikutty Edathi was sitting on the veranda and stitching a tear on the edge of her mundu. 'What news, Kalyanikutty Amma?' Kittunni Nair had folded back his mundu and tied his other mundu round his waist. Whenever he set out to do anything important Kittunni Nair would fold back his mundu and tie the other one round his waist.

'Finished all your work? All the rest must be asleep. Why don't you come to the building near the tank?' Kittunni Nair moved near Kalyanikutty Edathi and looked around before he put his hand on her arm. He said softly, 'Come, nothing will happen'. Kalyanikutty Edathi just turned around and gave a him a glare with burning eyes. Kittunni Nair wondered if he was facing Kalyanikutty

Amma or Bhadrakali herself. He had never faced this kind of reaction before. He felt that he would be burnt to a cinder if he stayed near her. Kittunni Nair could still feel that heat when he thought of Kalyanikutty Edathi. Kittunni Nair went to the pond, washed his face and feet and went to the fields as though to look at the work that was being done there. He did not count it a failure. Let her fall if she will, was his calculation.

Kalyanikutty Edathi did not speak of Kittunni Nair's invitation to the building near the pond to anyone. If she spoke of it, they would all blame her. They would say, 'Why would he try to flirt with you, if you didn't give him any encouragement?' She consoled herself with the thought that this would have happened because of the way the family had been talking of her these past days. Even if Kittunni Nair had done something, they were quite likely to have said, 'Who asked you to stay there and let him touch you?'

Nine

She felt better when she thought that she was not alone in this fate, there were others who suffered the like her in other households. Pazhedath Thankamani too, like her, had not been born the first or the last. One day when she came back from college and was changing, she happened to recite a couple of lines which went, 'How could a father and mother object to the beloved daughter's love?' Her father heard this and called out, 'What did you say? How can a father and mother object, is it?' He had absolutely no idea about poetry or literature. 'I'll show you. Don't get up to any mischief. Don't try to enact a love scene, all right?'

Thankamani was studying in the first year of the intermediate course. They did not let her complete the second year. They married her off to a Malayali from Bangalore called Hariharan. He was an accountant. Though Thankamani's wedding was conducted without asking her opinion, Kalyanikutty Edathi consoled herself with the thought that Thankamani had escaped. The wedding was performed very quickly without much fanfare. Her elder sister Parvathi's wedding had been celebrated grandly. They had brought down the famous cook Dasaratha Iyer from Thrithamara village. The nadaswara vidwan Ramaswami had been brought by taxi from Palghat by Raman Nair. There was a huge pandal on the eastern side of the house. Three huge fires had been built for cooking. Gramaphone music played from two days before the wedding. Balagopal who stayed in the next house was in charge of that.

Kalyanikutty Edathi had noticed all that. She wondered how her marriage would be celebrated. And then told herself that celebrated would be the wrong word, conducted was perhaps the right one. Saudamini Edathi's marriage had been even grander than Parvathi's. Ouseph from Trichur had been brought to make the pandal and decorate it. The mangalapatram which Kochuraman Master wrote that day still hung in the front hall. The bridegroom's name was written on the left and the bride's on the right, with the picture of a coconut tree in the middle. At the bottom it was written, 'With best wishes from Kochuraman Nair.' It also said, 'May the bride and groom be blessed by the goddess of love.' The wedding had taken place eight years back. There were five payasams and four types of fried stuff. The big papad was so large that it could cover the whole plantain leaf on which the rice was served. The bridegroom came with two bundles of thick white cloth, an umbrella and a huge trunk box. Their servant who came carrying the box was given lunch at the same time as the rest of the bridegroom's party, but he was seated slightly away from the rest. A second class citizen in the bridegroom's party. When he finished his lunch and went away, they gave him a bundle of tobacco leaves and some arecanuts. He wrapped them up and also the chips that were served for lunch.

Kalyanikutty Edathi did not dream about the man who would marry her, or about the way in which the wedding would be conducted. There was no point in dreaming about anything. And anyway, there was no time either. Since the women who came to work were of lower castes they could not enter the kitchen. They would sweep the yard and bring water from the well. The days they did not come, Kalyanikutty Edathi had to draw water from the well. She consoled herself with the thought that no one asked her to sweep the yard as well.

Saudamini Edathi and Vanaja were fair. Kalyanikutty Edathi was darker than them. They called her darky in fun when they were young and to hurt when they grew older. Kalyanikutty Edathi did not get mad with them. She did not feel jealous of her sisters either. She would console herself with the thought, 'It isn't anything I did.' It was not her fault after all that she was dark. Both her father and mother had not been fair. Ammini who lived next door was very fair.

'She has a white woman's colour.'

'She looks so good!'

'Wonder where she got this complexion that no one else in the family has.'

'Lovely dark hair too.'

That village saw a very fair complexion as an essential part of beauty. Anyone who brought a wedding proposal asked immediately, 'Is the girl fair?' If you said that she was not too fair, the interest level would immediately go down. The next step is to compare the complexion of the bride-to-be with that of others known to both.

Where men were concerned a fair complexion did not matter so much. Among other qualifications, this would also count as one. If the man was well-born and the horoscopes matched well, this would not matter.

'Thekkeparambil Narayanan Nair is lucky. All four of his children are fair.

He'll be able to find husbands for all of them quickly.' He and his wife were fair. But fate had to be on your side too. Just being born of a good family and being fair were not enough.

'Look at what happened to Narayanan Nair's eldest daughter. They married her off to a fair chap, from a good family. And what happened? The third day after she was taken to her husband's house, the girl was back here.'

'I'm not going back.' Her husband did not come in search of her either.

Gopalan knew why she had come back. 'It isn't Thankamani's fault that she had to come back,' Gopalan said.

'What's wrong with him? Does he have another establishment there or something?'

'What do you know? The question does not arise.' Gopalan declared. The usage wasn't original. He'd heard someone say that before.

If only Kalyanikutty Edathi could escape from all this. I prayed for someone to come with a proposal.

Good for nothing, whore, fast female – so many epithets were used to describe her. No one called her these names. But they asked, 'Where is that good for nothing?' or said, 'She's a fast female' and she heard these comments from inside the kitchen. Whenever she heard any of these words, her ears echoed with the word 'whore'. All the words used to describe her reached her ear in the form of that one word. How long would she need to suffer all this and live on? There was no answer. There was no one to help her find the answer. No one came forward to give her any advice either.

One day, a proposal came for her. Appukuttan, the bride-groom to be, was from Kozhikode. The women from his family came because the hororscopes matched very well. He was not from a very good family, but it was decided that that would do for Kalyanikutty Edathi.

One Tuesday evening, Appukuttan, another man and two women from his family came to the house. Kumarettan welcomed them and seated them in chairs on the verandah. A vessel of water had been kept on the edge of the veranda earlier for the guests to wash their feet. The other man was Appukuttan's uncle. The women went inside. The men sat and talked on the verandah. Kalyanikutty Edathi was asked to bring the tea. Kalyanikutty Edathi felt there was something wrong. Kumarettan asked Kalyanikutty Edathi 'You've put enough sugar haven't you?' and asked the visitors, 'You do take sugar, don't you?' in order to keep her there for a while.

Kalyanikutty Edathi realised what it was all about only when she went in after serving the tea. She'd not had a good look at Appukuttan. If he liked her, no one was going to ask her if she liked him. She'd been asked to take the tea to the front room only so that she could be seen. If they'd warned her earlier, she could at least have dressed better. They must have thought that it would be a good thing if someone would marry her and take her away. Who knew what the family thought. Anyway, she was a whore, wasn't she? If someone would marry her and take her away, that much less burden for the family. If not, she could work herself to death in the house. She had acted in one play now. She wondered how many more would be required. There were other creatures in the neighbouring houses who shared her fate, she consoled herself with that thought. And prayed that she would be born as an only child in her next birth at least.

The women who had come with Appukuttan did not look happy. Kumarettan and the others noticed that. After some time they only said, 'We'll make a move then.' That meant that the reaction was negative. As they went away, one of the women said, 'The girl is dark, one can't even say brown complexioned.'

'She's darker than Appukuttan.'

'I think she's as tall as he is.'

'Appukuttan had always wanted a fair bride, haven't you Appukuttan?'

'Wonder why the broker made us go all the way there when he knew this. Next time, we'll specifically ask about the girl's colour before we go. You can't make out anything from photographs.'

'It isn't as though there are no fair women in the land. And to take us there to see this one. Let that broker come again. I'll tell him not to step into this house with another proposal like this. It isn't difficult to get hold of a girl like this. There are some girls like that who work in the same place as Appukuttan. And to go and see one like this. Phoo!'

When the proposal petered out the blame fell on Kalyanikutty Edathi as usual.

'Who'll marry her?'

'They were polite enough not to get up and go when she took them the tea.'

No proposals came for a while. She was thirty two now. Vanaja was also growing older. If no proposals came for Kalyanikutty Edathi they could start looking for a husband for Vanaja.

'Why should she too grow old like this?'

'How can you marry off the younger sister when the elder's still at home and not married? One has to look at convention.'

'Does that mean Vanaja should never be married?'

The discussions about Kalyanikutty Edathi continued.

'I don't mind at all. Don't spoil anyone's future for my sake.' Kalyanikutty Edathi felt like telling them. But she did not say that. No one would pay any heed in any case. Anyway, Vanaja's marriage was fixed without much delay.

Vanaja's wedding was also

celebrated grandly as Saudamini Edathi's had been. The bridegroom Prabhakaran Nair was a good looking young man. Healthy-looking too.

'He'll suit Vanaja, she's so smart.'

Prabhakaran was employed at Kolar. In a gold mine there. His boss was a dark fat Tamilian. He was very fond of Prabhakaran. 'As long as he does not become too fond of Vanaja', at least some of the people thought.

'Prabhakaran'll cover her with gold.'

'Lucky to get a man who mines gold!' her friends teased Vanaja. Vanaja dreamt of gold rather than a married life. All she had were four bangles and a pair of earrings. Vanaja wondered if she would get a Lakshmi necklace for the wedding. She would have liked one.

A big rain-proof pandal was erected for Vanaja's wedding. Since it was the rainy season this precaution was necessary to prevent the rainwater from falling in the yard. Huge vessels were placed in strategic points to collect the rainwater that flowed through the semi-circular pipes on the roof of the pandal. The workmen were instructed to pour out the water that filled the vessels through the compound into the fields. The wedding was celebrated so grandly as though there would not be another wedding in the family.

Kalyanikutty Edathi was happy at her younger sister's marriage. Vanaja would now go to Kolar with her husband. Kalyanikutty Edathi was not mean enough to be happy that there would be one person the less to order her about. She only thought that Vanaja at least would now be happy. Vanaja had been very demanding, calling her every few minutes and wanting things done.

'I'm feeling so tired, will you wash these clothes for me?' she would say and dump all her dirty clothes on Kalyanikutty Edathi. Kalyanikutty Edathi had never said she would not wash them. And if, at any time, she had said so, the others would have yelled. 'Vanaja wasn't feeling well and so she asked her to wash her clothes as a favour. And this good for nothing did not help her!' that would be the reaction. She would no longer be troubled by Vanaja's demands. But she felt sad that her sister was going away from home.

Pathiraveettil Chandramathi was Kalyanikutty Edathi's classmate. They were friends as well. Would sit next to each other in class and talk during the breaks. Kalyanikutty Edathi would help Chandramathi who was weak in maths. She completed her intermediate only because of Kalyanikutty Edathi's help. Kalyanikutty Edathi would keep her answer paper in such a way that Chadramathi could see what was written on it. Chandrasekharan Master was aware of this, but did not comment because he had a fondness of Chandramathi. And she was rather fond of him. But Kalyanikutty Edathi did not feel jealous of that either. Chandrasekharan Master was transferred to Cherukunnu High School and Chandramathi was stuck in South Malabar. Those days love could not travel such distances. Transport was difficult. There were hardly any telephones. Letters took a long time to reach. How could 'love win all'? Master also erased all thoughts of that small love affair from his mind and consoled himself with the thought that there was a next birth when lovers could unite.

She had seen Chandrasekharan Master after a long while with his wife. Kalyanikutty Edathi did not compare the lives of Chandrasekharan and Chandramathi and herself, or waste time thinking of what might have been.

Chadramathi's wedding was fixed. The bridegroom was from Kottayam. The wedding was to be celebrated grandly. The family came in force to invite our family. Chandramathi came separately and spent a lot of time talking to Kalyanikutty Edathi. Kalyanikutty Edathi decided what she would wear when she went to the wedding. Vanaja's sari was better than her own. The blouse would fit her too. But she wasn't sure that she would get it if she asked for it and so decided not to ask at all. She would wear the best one she had.

But all that proved to be unnecessary. Everyone got ready to go, including Kalyanikutty Edathi. 'Saudamini's son has to go to school today for some function. Who'll give him food and send him off?' Everyone else looked at Kalyanikutty Edathi. She felt that it was better to volunteer before being ordered to stay and said, 'I'll take care of him.' She had destroyed so many wishes, not dreamt so many dreams. She heard all the details of her friend's wedding from others.

'Why didn't Kalyanikutty come?' Chandramathi asked. 'She'd some... Your earrings look good. They suit the sari.' Kalyanikutty Edathi heard about the sari Chandramathi wore, her jewellery, the feast that had been prepared. She got all the details up to the time Chandramathi was escorted to the bedroom and given milk and plantains by her relatives. Kalyanikutty Edathi did not even have the time to sit and think about those things in detail.

Ten

It was a year after Vanaja's wedding and after she had given birth to a child that Kalyanikutty Edathi received a proposal from K. N. Menon.

'The horoscopes match. The only thing is, he's from the South.'

'He's dark.'

'As if Kalyanikutty's complexion is like gold!'

'There's no point in waiting like this. Don't forget she's thirty five years old now.'

'Wait any longer and she'll never have children.'

'For whom are we waiting, royalty or something?'

'It's his second marriage.'

'It isn't as though he divorced his first wife. She ran away with someone else.'

'Have you asked Kalyanikutty?'

'That's great! Did anyone ask Saudamini and Vanaja before their marriages were fixed?'

'They say he has a child in his first marriage.'

'Yes, we heard he has a child. But the child is with the mother in England or France or some place like that.

'What about the wife?'

'With some white man. This man was lucky she didn't leave the girl behind for him to look after.'

'The child is with the mother. She's studying in England...'

'He doesn't have any other problems.'

'Then, let's fix this.'

The discussion about the proposal ended there.

'If the people find out that this is a second marriage...'

'Just keep quiet. You don't have to publish the news about this being a second marriage.'

'He's ten years older than her, that's all. Age doesn't count where men are concerned.'

Kalyanikutty Edathi's wedding was not celebrated very grandly, 'We'll just invite close relatives for the function.'

'We can hold it in July.'

'That's quite far away. Since it is fixed why not hold it sooner?'

Kalyanikutty Edathi did not know all this. No one told her either. 'What's the point in telling her about all this?' Invitations were printed.

'No need to spend a lot of money. It's a second marriage after all.'

No one remembered that it was not Kalyanikutty Edathi's second marriage. Nobody bothered to think of all that.

It was Gopikuttan who wrote the addresses on the covers and sent the invitations. He had a good handwriting.

The invitation cards used for Saudamini Edathi's and Vanaja's weddings had the picture of Ganapati on them. Gopikuttan had cut out one of them and pasted the picture on his table. The invitations were printed on thick paper. Kalyanikutty Edathi's invitations were printed on paper as thin as the cinema notices. Gopalan came running after some of the invitations had been sent off, ' How many have you sent already? Don't send off the rest.' Everyone got worried. 'There's a mistake in the invitation. Wedding has been typed as Weeding'. Since they did not know to whom invitations had already been despatched, it was decided to send the corrected invitations to everyone. 'Something's sure to go wrong where she is concerned.'

As if it was Kalyanikutty Edathi's fault that there had been a printing error in the wedding invitation.

Even the garlands that the bride and groom exchanged had to suffer. For Vanaja's and Saudamini's weddings, huge garlands made of jasmine had been arranged.

'Just get two garlands that have been used to decorate the deity in the temple. Tell that Varasyar who makes the garlands to make them slightly larger than usual.' And that decided the issue of the garlands for the wedding.

The wedding was celebrated very simply. The bridegroom's people also did not insist on a grand celebration. When Kalyanikutty Edathi went to the temple in the morning of the wedding it was Rajalakshmi from the next house who went with her. No one from her house went. When she had gone to another slightly distant temple earlier, it was Dakshayani, the daughter of the maid Paru, who had accompanied her. Wonder what Kalyanikutty Edathi prayed for. It must have been for release. Release from what? She did not even know to which world she was to go.

K. N. Menon came, accompanied by a party of forty people. They reached the bride's place one and a half hours before the muhurtam. The guests who were already there got acquainted with the bridegroom's people. Some people just looked at them. The women who had gathered tried to peer through the windows and find out what the bridegroom looked like.

'It must be the man with the moustache. He is wearing a mundu with a kasavu border.'

'It can't be him. He's completely bald. You can see your face on his head.'

'It must be the man in the other kasavu mundu. The kasavu border is quite two inches broad.'

'That is the bridegroom's elder brother.'

'He's not bald.'

'Baldness is not infectious.'

'Why do you want to guess when you are going to find out within a short time.'

The bridegroom and his people reached the gate. There was a man carrying a suitcase and carrying an umbrella with them. He was a servant at K. N. Menon's house. He was wearing a white shirt and mundu which K. N. Menon had bought him. He looked impressive in them.

The record player was belting out film songs even before the bridegroom's party reached. Nadaswaram had been played for the earlier two weddings. And they had gone to Trichur to buy gold two weeks before the wedding. None of this had happened at this wedding. 'Ask Saudamini to give her a good sari. She's her sister, after all.' Though Saudamini Edathi did not look too happy about it, she agreed to give a sari. She didn't ask whether Kalyanikutty Edathi liked the sari she had chosen before she gave it. Kalyanikutty Edathi also did not say. 'This sari is a nice one' or 'That one'll suit me better.'

The gramaphone sang, 'Come my friends, come my friends, hear this story,' a song from the movie Jnanambika, making some of the guests laugh. Some of the elders looked sternly at Ramachandran who was in charge of changing the records.

Kalyanikutty Edathi was led to the pandal escorted by her aunt, Saudamini Edathi and three or four others. Saudamini Edathi was wearing an expensive Benares silk sari. Vanaja wore a kasavu sari with a golden border which was quite six inches broad. Kalyanikutty Edathi did not try any comparisons. Anyone who did not know the family would think that Vanaja was the day's bride. The grand clothes worn by her sisters did not trouble Kalyanikutty Edathi. Nor did the fact that only one payasam was served at her wedding. Just a payasam in milk. Two payasams as well as a thick jaggery and ghee payasam had been served at the earlier two weddings.

No one outside the family knew that it was the bridegroom's second marriage. No one asked anything about it either. But when you looked at the scale of the celebrations, it looked as though it was Kalyanikutty Edathi's second marriage.

Kalyanikutty Edathi got up early from her bridal chamber and went to the pond for a bath. She changed and came to the veranda after tying up her hair. Everyone looked at Kalyanikutty Edathi with sarcastic smiles as though she had been up to some mischief.

It was Muthassi who broke the silence. 'Kalyani, did you sleep well?' That gave everyone a chance to snigger. It was not that they did not know better to ask whether the bride had slept well on her first night. It was just that they did not know what else to ask her.

'What's for breakfast?' As usual that day too, the question was addressed to Kalyanikutty Edathi. She had also not expected to be relieved of her daily duties, just because she had got married the previous day. Someone would surely say, 'Just because she's got married, does that mean that no one need eat here.' Kalyanikutty Edathi got a chance to act like a bride only when she came to the pandal as a bride and the thali was tied. Even at that time, Kalyanikutty Edathi's thoughts had not been of a honeymoon or the first night or anything of that sort. She was wondering what other roles she would have to play in her life.

She knew that that night this machine would have to submit to new experiments, that she would have to give herself up to new experiences which might be pleasant or unpleasant. She did not have any dreams or expectations other than that.

The others would have comments.

'She wouldn't have slept last night.'

'Say that he wouldn't have let her sleep.'

'He's experienced, isn't he?'

'She's not bad either. She's read more books on all this than most people.'

'Her eyes looked as though she had not slept at all.'

Kalyanikutty Edathi knew that all sorts of comments were being passed behind her back. As far as she was concerned, she only felt that another day had dawned. She had felt lonely last night too. She had yielded to the demands of a stranger, she felt. As she yielded in all matters at home, that night too she had yielded to another person's will. She would now have extra duties, those of a wife as well. If she did not do her usual work she would have to listen to complaints about that. She took up an extra burden silently.

'Kalyanikutty, is the bath water hot yet?' that was Kumarettan's voice.

K. N. Menon got up a little later. He drank the tea that Kalyanikutty Edathi brought and smoked a couple of cigarettes before he came out.

Kalyanikutty Edathi went to the kitchen to make dosa and chutney for breakfast. K. N. Menon spent the time thinking of other things. His mind was not on that house and its surroundings.

Mousumi had run away with Johnson when Mini was two years old. He had married Mousami when he had been working in Pune. The Chairman of the company he had been working in, the Managing Director and some of the other local bigwigs had attended the function. The Company chairman had thrown a huge cocktail party the night before the wedding. The party went on till dawn. Mousami's father was a retired Army officer and he was particular that his only daughter's wedding should be noticed by everyone, should be a topic of conversation for a long time after it was over. Slim Mousumi floated around at the party. She was dressed in modern fashion, with practically her whole back exposed. Her dangling earrings were as large as two large bangles. As Mousumi talked, they swung this way and that. That night everyone wanted to dance with the heroine of the night. Each of them danced with her and then kissed her. The Brigadier too danced with a lot of women. K. N. Menon was immersed in listening to the other guests congratulating him on his good fortune.

'Lucky guy!'

'What a sport!'

'Have a nice honeymoon.'

'Don't forget to come to the Club with her.'

All of them congratulated him. The congratulations offered by some people with long views, held hints of their own desires.

On the wedding day, Mousumi and K. N. Menon reached their bridal chamber about two o'clock in the night. The rituals and the reception had gone on till then. The smell of jasmine was all-pervading. Both of them could not remember what happened after that. The previous night's drinking and the lack of sleep for two nights made them both fall into the bed and sleep like logs. It was only early in the morning that they remembered that it was their first night. They did not waste time in regrets but started celebrating the night till it dawned and long after it dawned as well.

Mousumi had been a centre of attraction right from her college days. A number of her classmates had pursued her for dates. She had not gone steady with anyone. She had participated in a fashion show on the day of the college anniversary. The clothes she wore that day had been a topic of conversation for months on end and not only in the college. She had worn a sleeveless top with hot pants. As she walked the ramp all parts of her body were in motion. When she bowed at the end of the show at least some of the audience wondered if the neck need have been cut so low. Some of the others enjoyed it, of course.

A number of men had proposed to Mousumi and been rejected. Her logic was that she was not old enough for the shackles of marriage and this age was meant to be enjoyed. Even after the marriage, Mousumi used to go out with her old friends. But she had changed her logic. One eats every day at home. Still, once in a while, eating out is fun. Mousumi enjoyed that kind of change in all things.

Mousumi had been friendly with Johnson who was the Chief Engineer in the Company even before her marriage. They used to go out for lunch or dinner together once in a while.

The friendship continued after her marriage as well. She used to visit Johnson once in a while. Menon was not aware of what happened in his absence as her life was anyway involved with the Club and card parties. Even after Mini was born that relationship continued. Menon did have some suspicions. Some nights Mousumi would return home after dinner. They would come together very late after having dined together. Johnson had divorced his wife and was settled in Pune. But Menon did not expect that he would run away with Mousumi.

Menon did not really mind Mousumi's going away. But he could not bear the fact that she had taken Mini away. The thoughts of his daughter could reduce him to silence always. Where was she now? She must have grown a lot. Mousumi was cruel. Mini must be aware of that. He hoped that his daughter had inherited more of his character than that of her mother. There was no point in blaming the white man. It was all because of her. Would she have left Johnson as well? The father in Menon could not forgive her, ever.

Thoughts about Mini had often prompted him to drink. To forget his daughter, to stop thinking about

Mousumi, he often needed a couple of drinks.

But such things might cause talk in this village. He did not know how Kalyanikutty who lay next to him, with whom he was barely acquainted, would see these things. It took some time for Kalyanikutty to understand that her husband needed a couple of pegs every evening if he was to sleep. She had the endurance to put up with that as well. Her husband also viewed her as a machine. She was expected to see him in that way as well. This was the thought that kept disturbing her.

Eleven

Menon knew that the relationship between Mousumi and Johnson was not innocent. He also knew there was no point in advising or yelling at Mousumi. He felt that it was better to suffer the indignity in silence in the interests of his own peace of mind and peace in the family. He had often felt that Mousumi had married him just so that she could call herself someone's wife. She could go her own way behind the cover of respectability that the title gave her. Otherwise people would call her fast. A husband was just an address as far as Mousumi was concerned. A good-looking young man. An executive in a reputable concern. She had married him to use that reputable front to cover her own wanderings.

Menon had noticed even before they were married that Mousumi was seductive in her behaviour with most men. She was very stingy where wearing clothes was concerned. Her wish was to parade her undoubted charms whenever she went out and so be the cynosure of all eyes. He had believed that she would change after her marriage, that she would show proper respect for her new status, but that turned out to be a vain hope. He had to recognize that Mousumi would never change. Her life was dedicated to being a social butterfly fitting between club and home and parties.

Soon after Menon went to office in the morning, Mousumi would also go out. Most days she would not have got out of bed when he left for office. She would be dozing in the hangover from the previous night's dancing and boozing. It was only on Sundays that she had breakfast with him. Her evenings were spent at the club or at parties at friends' houses. Menon too liked partying and socializing. But he soon grew to realise that Mousumi did not have a life other than this. As far as she was concerned, looking after the house was a job meant for servants. She left the day to day running of the house to the servants and the supervision to Menon.

Her relationship with Johnson started troubling Menon. He wondered where the whole thing was heading, but he knew that he had no way of controlling Mousumi. Once Johnson had to go to Goa on work. He suggested that Mousumi accompany him so that she could see the place. Menon had no difficulty in guessing that it was Mousumi who had given him the courage to suggest such a thing to him. He could see the shadow of a conspiracy in the request. If he did not permit her to go there would be no peace in the house after that. They went to Goa for four days. It was certain that they did not see the place at all. They would have hardly stirred out of their room. They were celebrating their own 'honeymoon'. They came back after spending time with each other in absolute freedom. Menon did not even ask her what the Goa trip had been like. Johnson told Menon when they met at the office, 'Your wife is really great, she's great company.'

It wasn't that Menon did not understand what he was being told. He wondered if Johnson could read from his face what he felt.

Menon was unwilling to initiate a confrontation. Since he obviously did not possess some of the qualities and abilities that Johnson had, he kept his peace. He decided that it was better to appear unmoved.

One day, he forgot to take a paper when he went to the office. Normally, he returned home only in the evening. Lunch was usually with the other executives in the company.

That day, when he returned home unexpectedly, he saw Johnson's car parked a little distance away from the gate. There was no driver in the car. If the man had been there, he could have asked him where Johnson had gone.

When Menon rang the doorbell, it took a little while for the door to be opened. Mousumi opened the door with the expression on her face asking the question who had come to disturb her at this odd hour. She did not know how to react when she saw who had rung the bell. Her hair was all awry and her makeup smeared. Menon went in without a word and picked up the paper he had come for. He did not even glance at their bedroom before he returned. Johnson also returned after he got what he had come for. Don't worry, nothing will happen, Mousumi consoled him. Menon knew his colleague even better than Mousumi did. Johnson would just argue that this had not happened in his house, he was an invited guest in Menon's house.

That was one of the rare occasions when Mousumi had felt fear. What would happen when Menon returned in the evening? What could she say? Either he would throw her out of the house or he would kill her. There was nothing she could say in her own defence. She had been caught red-handed, beyond the need for any further evidence or testimony. He could have rung up before he came. True, he had not come expecting to find her in a compromising situation. He would not have expected to see what he did see. She had never wanted a life with Johnson. She had only viewed Johnson as a machine which could satisfy her extreme needs. She knew from experience that Johnson had capabilities which no other man in her acquaintance did. Johnson had stayed in the house often when Menon was on tour. Both of them had bodies which were insatiable. Menon could never compete with Johnson where that was concerned.

Mousumi did not know how she spent the day till Menon came home in the evening. She did not feel like ringing up friends for long chats on the telephone or going out for shopping trips. She tried to take a nap in the afternoon. She could not sleep. She could only guess at the development and the ending of the plot, the first scene of which had been played in the morning. Anything could happen.

Menon too spent his time in the office under great tension. His wife and his colleague... He did not know at whom his anger was directed. No point in blaming the guy, if she had not been the kind of woman she is, he would have left her alone, he thought. After a while he would think, what is the point in blaming her, he is the kind of chap who can't leave any woman alone. He could not do any work that day. Just sat and smoked cigarette after cigarette.

'How come, Menon?'

'Just like that.'

He did not normally eat in the office canteen. That day, unusually, he went to the canteen for lunch. He also took along his colleague Balraj. They spent some time over lunch talking of all sorts of subjects. Balraj noticed that there was something wrong with Menon.

'Are you all right? Sickening for flu or something of that sort?'

'Nothing like that. But I do feel out of sorts.'

Balraj did not know why Menon had invited him for lunch. He did know a little of Mousumi's reputation and wondered if this strange mood had something to do with her. But he was certain that this was not the time for any enquiries.

The previous Saturday, Menon and Mousumi and Balraj had met at the Club. Johnson had been late that evening. It was twelve by the time he reached. The usual round of drinking and dancing went on. After a while Menon got up to go home.

'Mousumi, shall we make a move?'

'Don't worry, I'll drop her home if you want to leave early.'

Balraj also said he'd stay for some more time. His wife had gone to their hometown. Menon too felt that there was nothing wrong in leaving Mousumi there since it was not just Johnson, but Balraj too was there for company. But after a while, Balraj had left. It was two in the night when Johnson dropped Mousumi home.

'Why are you so late?' Menon asked his wife.

'Don't worry, darling, it was a nice evening,' was the only reply Mousumi vouchsafed him. Since the smell of liquor laced her breath, he did not ask anything further.

Menon once again thought of the trip Mousumi had taken to Goa in Johnson's company. Why had they gone? And why had he given his permission for that trip? Was it because she would have gone even if he hadn't given his permission. He had given her too much license. It would not be right to put all the blame on her. He too had contributed to the situation. Still...

He had not questioned her when she returned from Goa. He did not ask her how the trip had been. Nor had she volunteered anything on the topic. Balraj had asked him that day, 'Why didn't you go along too?' Why had Balraj asked that? Did Balraj also have an idea of the relationship between Mousumi and Johnson?

Menon used to go for many parties after his marriage. He always took his wife along. In fact one could say that he got many of the invitations he did because he was married to Mousumi. Even if he was reluctant to go, Mousumi would insist. Once in a while, if he resisted, she would go alone. To begin with, he had been happy to escort Mousumi to all these parties. He felt that he was the cynosure of all eyes when he went accompanied by his wife. Though the people who came and greeted them spoke more to Mousumi, Menon liked that attention.

Mousumi wondered whether she should ring Menon at the office. She picked up the telephone once or twice. After a few moments she put it back in its cradle. What could she tell him over the telephone? How could she start? Suppose he just put down the telephone when he heard her voice? He might just explode. She did not know what to do. It might be better just to keep quiet for the moment. Even if he was really wild now, he might have cooled down a little by the evening. There was no point in fanning the flames by talking to him now.

She bathed much later than usual. She spent a lot of time in the bathroom that day. She poured buckets of water over herself. As if she was trying to wash off something. But her sense of guilt did not wash off. Her head ached. After a while she came and lay on the bed. She got up almost immediately and tried to read a book. The pages would not turn.

Some time later, Susan John rang up. Her husband K. K. John was a very rich man. They entertained a lot. Mousumi was always invited. Menon was not very fond of the company. Drinking and dancing went on till all hours of the night. Most days, Mousumi would go alone and come back unsteady on her legs. Menon would be fast asleep by then.

'Mousumi, aren't you coming for the usual card game?' Susan asked. We're planning to play 56 today. You like that better don't you? We have a new guest today. Sandip Menon. His new movie is coming out next week. He's good company.'

Mousumi did not pay much attention. 'Not today, Susan.'

'That is not like you. What happened?'

'I'm not in the mood for it. A slight headache.'

'The curse?'

'No, it isn't that.'

Susan did not press her after that. She had hardly put down the telephone when the next call came. It was Rita Menon this time.

'Mousumi, I'm going to Bannerjee's. Why don't you come along. We'll have lunch there and return immediately. His wife and family are not here.'

Mousumi normally liked going to Bannerjee's house. But she did not feel like it today.

'Not today, Rita.'

'What's got into you?'

'I'll tell you later.'

Susan John rang up Rita Menon, 'Rita, did you speak to Mousumi today?'

'I did. She seems to be in a peculiar mood.'

'I thought so too.'

'Did you find out what's wrong with her?'

'She didn't say. When I pressed her she just said she'd tell me later.'

'Maybe, she has a visitor,' there was mischief in Rita's voice.

'I don't think so. She'd be on a high if that was so.'

'She has a regular. He might be coming. She claims she has learnt a lot from him.'

'I don't think that's the reason today.'

'We'll try her after a day or so.'

Mousumi did not feel angry with Johnson for having put her in such a position. The time she spent with him only made her feel better. But today, it was Menon who filled her thoughts.

Menon was a little late from office. As each minute passed, Mousumi started getting more and more nervous. Menon's face, however, showed no emotion at all. As he sat and had his tea, Mousumi was watching his face for any change of expression. She was watching out for a movement from the tongue, the hands. His silence only disturbed her further. Couldn't he say something, yell at her, beat her, anything. Mousumi could not understand the meaning of his silence. She could not help thinking that a husband who did not react at all even when he caught his wife with her lover could hardly be called a husband. But the time for confrontation had not yet been exhausted. There was still time for accusations and apologies. She could tender an apology and declare herself willing to accept any punishment, only if an accusation was made. This silence was an unbearable punishment. She could not take the initiative. If she said, 'Forgive me', and fell at his feet, that might set off the eruption of a volcano. She did not even think of going to the Club that evening. She had an early supper and went and lay down on the bed. Menon came to the bedroom a little later. When he moved towards the bed, Mousumi thought her end had come. Instead, the prowess and force he brought to sex that night shocked Mousumi. Mousumi who was quite willing to experiment sexually, and took part in all sorts of perversions quite willingly, felt as though she had been raped. Could this be the punishment she had been given? Menon had demonstrated that he was even better than Johnson. He had changed into a machine which went through the whole exercise with no emotion or tenderness. Mousumi could not understand how her husband had developed all this strength and ferocity suddenly. Afterwards, Menon moved away without a word, without even a sigh. Mousumi did not have the courage to touch him or to ask him anything. Both the characters in the drama got up in complete silence.

Who was this new man? Where had he been all this while? Where did he find such strength suddenly? She did not get any reply. Mousumi wondered in this had been the punishment given by him. He must have thought he'd teach her a lesson. She had seen the lava of his revenge pour out. Though she did not claim that she was innocent of any crime, she was helpless before him. He had cornered her and punished her without giving her a chance to beg his forgiveness or offer him an explanation. And what a punishment! What a lesson!

Mousumi knew that she would never again see this particular incarnation of her husband. Menon withdrew into his old self. Mousumi could not understand him. How long could she live with him without understanding what made him the way he was. The 'Johnson' she had seen in Menon that night would never return. He had already had his revenge on her and Johnson. Who had won in the encounter – Johnson? Menon? she herself? Mousumi did not get the answer to that question.

That incident must have prompted her to elope with Johnson. Mousumi carried the burden of that night in her life with Johnson after that.

Twelve

When Kalyanikutty Edathi was taken to her husband's house the day after the wedding none of the family appeared sad about the parting. Kalyanikutty Edathi too did not suffer the pangs of separation. No one sighed, 'She's gone'. They must have been troubled by the thought that she would come back.

After a few days she would be taken to her husband's place of work. There might have been people in the family who prayed that would come to pass, not because they wanted her to live comfortably with him, but because they wanted to see the last of her.

Her aunt escorted her to her husband's house as was usual. Since her aunt wanted to see for herself what sort of a household K. N. Menon's was, she was not at all reluctant to take up the duty. There was a big reception and a feast arranged at that house. It didn't feel like a second marriage. As far as Menon's relatives were concerned this was the first wedding to be conducted in his own village. The women from neighbouring households and the relatives opened out a new world before Kalyanikutty Edathi, gave her experience of an atmosphere she was not familiar with. Everyone behaved as though they were willing to like her. They did not look critically at her and she too did not try to impress them with insincere behaviour. One could say that this was the one interval of peace and goodwill that Kalyanikutty Edathi experienced in her life. She did not have to wash even her own clothes. Her husband's niece combed her hair for her. Everyone came and spoke to her. Kalyanikutty Edathi had to try hard to lie to them and convince them that her life till then had also been pleasant. She kept wondering what life had in store for her from then on.

She could console herself with the thought that she would have to work only for her husband and herself wherever she was. Or she would have servants to help her. Kalyanikutty Edathi dreamt of a new world, a new atmosphere. Whatever it was like, she was sure it would be better than the hell she had been living in till then.

Gopikuttan came from home by then. Everyone got rather worried that something had happened in her house. But he had only brought along some clothes Kalyanikutty Edathi had forgotten to bring.

'She's always forgetful. Go give all this to her. Or she'll embarrass all of us in her husband's house.' That was how they sent him there. Though Gopikuttan had come to visit her in a strange house, Kalyanikutty Edathi was happy to see him. He stayed there that night and returned only the next morning. Kalyanikutty Edathi got a chance to sit and talk with him for a while. He was the only friend she had in her own house. It was Kalyanikutty Edathi who had taught him poetry and stories. He was the son of a relative. His parents had died when he was very young. He had been brought up in her house as a sort of unpaid help. But he was very bright.

That night, after the rest of the visitors had gone away, Kalyanikutty Edathi went up to their room with her husband. Since Gopikuttan had to leave early in the morning, before she would have come down, she said goodbye to him at night. She felt her eyes fill with tears. Gopikuttan too had moist eyes.

Kalyanikutty Edathi was once again alone in the new world with a husband who was a stranger and his people who were strangers. But there were no grumbles and scoldings and barked out orders in this new world. This interval would get over in another three or four days. She could not help thinking of that all the time.

The days spent at Menon's house were comparatively peaceful. Kalyanikutty Edathi had no problem in getting along with Menon's sisters and other relatives. She helped them with the housework.

'You don't have to work in the kitchen. We're here to do all this.'

'It's all right. I don't mind doing it,' Kalyanikutty Edathi behaved like a member of the household.

'New brooms.'

'Nothing of the sort, she isn't like that.'

Menon's people asked her about her household. When she stayed there, she spent more time with his sisters and others rather than with him. There too, he spent most of his time sitting on the front veranda and smoking. He did not go for visits to his wife's relatives.

Kalyanikutty Edathi had noticed how close Menon's sisters were to each other. Menon had just two sisters. If there had been a third one, she could perhaps have compared that household with hers.

Kalyanikutty Edathi consoled herself with the thought that if there had been a third one, her fate would have been similar to her own.

Once they went back to her place, she found that being married made no difference to her status in her own house. She started feeling scared that the indifference and contempt that characterised the family's behaviour to her would be reflected in their behaviour to her husband as well. It took only days to prove that her fears were not unrealistic. Comparisons with the husbands of her two sisters and loud and sarcastic comments made in her hearing went on all the time.

'Both Saudamini's and Vanaja's husbands have lots of hair. Vanaja's husband has thick dark and curly hair.'

'Her husband has only a line of hair as though someone had made a border round the bald patch.'

'He's dark and bald – really a suitable bridegroom.'

'I believe he's been bald since he was young.'

'Maybe there's nothing inside to make the hair grow out.'

'He was in the army before he got this job. I believe he lost his hair because he had to wear a cap all the time.'

K. N. Menon returned to Dubai where he worked. Menon was happy he had been asked to go to a new place from Pune where he had lived with Mousumi. Pune would spread out old memories before him and disturb him. Though the transfer was abroad, and his stay was not so comfortable, he was happy about it. He would be earning more as well. There were problems about taking your family. But by that time Menon had stopped feeling the need of the constant presence of a wife. He had got married again only because his people had insisted. Now he was responsible for looking after one more person. He performed his duties as a husband by sending money and parcels home.

After K. N. Menon returned to Dubai, every three months or so, large parcels would come for Kalyanikutty Edathi. The day the parcel came everyone in the house would gather round it and open it, taking out things one by one. Only Kalyanikutty Edathi, to whom it was addressed, would stay a little apart, as though she was saying 'I don't have any right over these things.' The others too would act as though the parcel had come to the whole household and what did she have to do with all these. The parcel would be treated as common property. It would contain toothpaste and shaving cream tubes, bottles of hair creams, soaps of different kind, all sorts of things like that. Gopalan had a story about one of the women who picked up a tube of shaving cream and tried to brush her teeth with it. Her defence was that she did not think Menon would send shaving cream to a household where there were no male members who shaved.

Once he sent an expensive sari. No one else in the place had such an expensive sari. Claimants rushed forward to wear it the first time. Saudaminiedathi and Vanaja and their cousins all had their eyes on the sari. Finally, Vanaja wore it the first time for a wedding. Kalyanikutty Edathi did not act as though it was something that belonged to her alone. There was no point in making such claims either.

When he came on leave, K. N. Menon did not get the kind of welcome that the husbands of the other girls in the family got. Kalyanikutty Edathi too had very little time to spend with her husband. She had so much work to do that she hardly had time to talk for a while with him. And both Menon and Kalyanikutty Edathi were not the type to snatch time for such conversations either. No one had seen them go to the temple or to the houses of relatives together. Menon did not believe in going to the temple at all.

'Oh, her guy has come. Wonder when the tea will get ready tomorrow,' Kalyanikutty Edathi could hear such comments from behind the walls.

Kalyanikutty Edathi never had the good fortune to accompany her husband to Dubai, or to stay with him in a house of their own, or even to run her own household as she liked. Even her married life was empty and lonely.

There was one night the whole of which she had spent in crying, lying on the floor. She could never forget what had happened. Whenever she thought of the incident again she would feel like sitting down somewhere and weeping. It was on the second day after she returned from her husband's house after the first visit.

'What's happened? Her eyes are red.'

'What did he do to make her cry like this?'

'She must be thinking of her fate.'

'What's the point? She could not have got a better husband anyway.'

'He would not have beaten her or anything.'

'He's not the type.'

'You know that Menon who's married the girl from Kurumbathu. He first pokes a lighted cigarette on his wife's arse and then...'

'Shut up.'

Kalyanikutty Edathi did not ever tell anyone why she had cried. All this only added to the burden of sorrow that she already carried in her mind.

No one enquired what had happened. Anyway, nobody every shared her sorrows or joys. Hers was one of those lives which were denied the right to sorrows and joys.

The discussion about Kalyanikutty Edathi's eyes being red ended there.

'If she doesn't want to tell anyone, let her suffer on her own.'

'She acts as though she doesn't have a tongue anyway.'

Where her family was concerned the

incident ended there. But for Kalyanikutty Edathi, it was unforgettable. She had wept over the incident a number of times. Whenever she felt the need to weep and let the tears ease her burden of grief she would think of that incident.

The day after she returned from her husband's house, her people took back the ornaments they had bought for her wedding. They had bought her a gold chain of two sovereigns and two pairs of gold bangles besides the gold chain that she used to wear. The ornaments had been purchased from Trichur. Kalyanikutty Edathi had not been taken along when the rest of the family went for shopping.

'She needn't come.'

'As if she knows to choose jewels!'

They acted as if the matter hardly concerned her. After all, if they could choose a husband, they could choose a chain and some bangles as well.

She had taken out the tali from the

thread it had been tied on and put it on the chain she habitually wore.

'Why do you need two gold chains?' The gold bangles too gave way to glass bangles. Kalyanikutty Edathi did not protest. Protest to whom? For what?

Kalyanikutty Edathi had earlier thought that the springs of her tears had dried up. When she thought of this incident, she realised that at least one spring still remained.

She did not show any resentment even then. She did not even feel that there was something odd in this cruelty. Did K. N. Menon notice what had happened? Kalyanikutty Edathi did not think about that either. If she felt that he realised what had happened and how upset she had been and had not offered to replace what had been lost, she would have felt even more miserable. She certainly did not speak to him of this. He did not seem to have noticed that glass bangles had replaced the gold ones. She did not even wonder how her family could do this to her. She just felt that this was the way she had to live.

'She's already found someone, hasn't she? Who is she going to parade before, wearing ornaments? If she wants to wear some, let her husband get her some.'

'That's not likely. He must have got fed up, buying ornaments for the first one.'

'Who's this one going to run away with? No one's likely to ask her, are they?'

She heard all the comments. And bore them in silence.

It was not as though she had longed for that extra gold chain or the bangles. She had not felt jealous when Vanaja and Saudaminiedathi wore two pairs of bangles on each hand and a chain of four sovereigns. She did not protest that the family had bought her only a chain of two sovereigns for her wedding.

When she was taken to Menon's

house after the wedding, his sisters saw that she was wearing only two bangles each on either hand. They had noticed, when they came with the proposal, that the other two sisters wore four bangles each on both hands. They did not comment on that.

'They are fonder of your sisters, aren't they?' Menon's elder sister asked her once.

Kalyanikutty Edathi did not try to cover up by saying that she did not like jewels or that she had kept aside a few. She did not say anything at all. She just listened.

She did not deserve anything, she felt. Not even a life. Her days were spent in labour for the comfort of others. Yet, that gold chain and the bangles stayed with her as a springwell of tears for ever.

Thirteen

Not long after the wedding, Menon had to stop staying in his own house. Even the few days that she stayed in his house were like other days to Kalyanikutty Edathi. She did not blame anyone else for the fact that she was not able to spend some time alone with him or talk with him alone. She did not curse her fate either. Even on their first night, there had been no feeling of sharing, perhaps because it was his second marriage. That was a beginning. There was nothing to awaken her emotions or needs, not even caresses. She had lain there like a machine that night. She felt that this was another joy that had been denied to her like other joys had been.

Menon had very limited needs. He would just sit quietly. He did not see his wife to speak to during the day. Food was served on time. Kalyanikutty Edathi had other things to do, she could not spend her time looking after the welfare of just one person.

Perhaps because he had been taken unawares by a sudden burst of affection, one day, when Kalyanikutty Edathi was hanging out clothes in the hall, Menon came that way and caught her to himself. The scene ended quickly when they heard someone's footsteps outside. Kalyanikutty Edathi often thought of that moment when she had felt unaccustomed joy. But what was the point? That was never repeated.

Menon came on leave from his job abroad only twice. Each time he'd come on one month's leave. Kalyanikutty Edathi had hoped that she would be able to stay with him for a few days at least in his own house. But she could stay there only two days. By the time Menon came on leave the second time, his family was in the midst of a terrible fight. Both his sisters had filed suits for the partition of the family property. Though they were still staying in the same house, they had separate kitchens by then. If Kalyanikutty Edathi went to one of the sisters, the other sister would disown her. When Menon was forced to live like a stranger in his own house, Kalyanikutty Edathi also had to suffer the same fate.

Menon's elder sister had started the talk of partitioning the family property, 'My children are growing up. We too want some land and a house of our own.'

'What's wrong with staying here. There aren't many people in this house and I'm sure you don't have any problems here.'

'My husband is retiring in a few months. He'll have to come and stay here. It's better that we live separately then.'

Some time earlier, she had gone and stayed at the place where her husband was working. She had taken a lot of things from the tharavad when she went there.

'I'm taking this with me.' Thankamaniamma, the elder sister said one day. She was talking of the carved bedstead on which their grandfather had lain. That bedstead was a beautiful one and seemed a symbol of the household's prosperity.

'It was made at the time of the Karyakkar.'

'No one else has slept on it.' When the bedstead was lifted down from the pathayapura, it was as though a dead body was being brought down.

Naturally, the second daughter also joined in the draining of the family home. 'If that is so, I too have my rights.' And she took away the huge bronze lamps as well as the copper and bronze vessels that were stored in the big granary.

Menon's mother said, 'No one is going to take it away when they go away for ever, are they? Let them take what they want. There's no need for anyone to fight over that.'

When the property was partitioned too, the sisters took all of it between them. Menon was given nothing.

'After his wedding, he hasn't bothered about us at all. He gave everything he earned to his wife,' was the excuse given.

Menon did not fight the partition He quietly settled down in his wife's house. He had no reason to expect a treatment different from what his wife got. But he bore everything stoically.

Menon had told Kalyanikutty Edathi that he would take her with him the next time he went abroad. 'There isn't any accommodation available just now.' One couldn't say that Kalyanikutty Edathi waited for the next time. She was losing her ability to dream little by little.

'The next time' never arrived. After one year, Menon returned with a hold-all and two suitcases. Everyone felt there was something wrong when they caught sight of the hold-all. K. N. Menon had never written about his job abroad, or the way he lived there. He would send money every month and Kalyanikutty

Edathi would hand it over for the household expenses.

All he said was, 'I'm not going back'. He did not say whether he'd given up his job and returned, whether he'd been sacked or anything. Even otherwise he rarely mentioned anything about his job to Kalyanikutty Edathi. Menon's return provided material for family conclaves.

'He must have been sacked.'

'But he's supposed to work very hard.'

'Wonder if he got into some other trouble.'

'He's not likely to have got involved in shady money dealings.'

'Lots of women working in his office...'

'He's not like that at all...'

The house acquired a new and permanent resident. Menon knew that it wasn't good to stay in his wife's house

for ever. He could not go and stay in his house. And renting a house in one's own or one's wife's village would cause talk.

'Complete rest from now on.'

'Can't he get some job?'

'Who'll give him a job in this village?'

'He could start a business.'

'One needs to be smart for that.'

Menon did not go over to his house at all. His sisters would probably have said, 'Why on earth did he have to come here?'

Kalyanikutty Edathi's household did not treat him any better. He did not get the consideration or respect that the husbands of the other two sisters got. They were employed. Though they did not contribute to the household expenses, they spent on their wives' needs.

Menon also, like Kalyanikutty Edathi, became an unwanted element in the family. His fate was to be unemployed and to live there eating food given by people who did not care about him, and to be ignored by them. All of them looked at him as though he was good for nothing.

Menon would sometimes go to the market. He would go the Panchayat library and sit and read the newspapers there. He would talk to the Postmaster Abraham and the tailor Kumaran Nair. He would return by noon.

One day, as he was about to leave the house for the library, he heard someone say from inside, 'If you're going to the market, please buy a pound of sugar.' He was given the money too. Slowly, such instructions grew more frequent. Menon did not grumble about it. He was used to going to the market and buying provisions. But he had not thought that he would have to do such things in this village. Menon and Kalyanikutty Edathi suffered all these indignities in silence. They did not even discuss this between themselves. Not only was

Menon not treated as well as the husbands of the other two sisters, he was losing what respect he used to get as well. Kalyanikutty Edathi did notice what was happening. Since Menon was not the kind of person to grumble about such things, there was no overt trouble. Both husband and wife found strength in being patient. Both of them were at par in this matter.

K. N. Menon did not have a job. He could not return to Dubai. He could not get another job in the village. He could only live in his wife's house. Another burden to Kalyanikutty, another curse on her.

Marriage had gifted Kalyanikutty Edathi with a son. This had happened the first time Menon came on leave. By the time he returned to Dubai that time, she had missed her periods. They had thought Menon would reach the village by the time the delivery date came by. But he could not reach since he was not granted leave.

It was the midwife Visalakshi who delivered Kalyanikutty Edathi's child. Saudaminiedathi took three days after the pain started to deliver her first child. The midwife warned the family that a doctor was needed and that she could not be responsible for the consequences if a doctor was not called. It was only then that Dr. Velayudhan Nair was called. Kalyanikutty Edathi did not wonder what would have happened to her if a similar warning had been given. A normal delivery was a boon given to her by god.

Menon came after a couple of weeks after the delivery. He had brought baby powder and dresses and toys for the child. Kalyanikutty Edathi did not show off because her child had more things than Saudaminiedathi's and Vanaja's children. She shared whatever had been brought. Vanaja delivered a couple of weeks after Kalyanikutty Edathi did.

Vanaja did not have breast milk. Kalyanikutty Edathi had so much that her blouse kept getting wet every now and then. She volunteered to feed Vanaja's child as well. Vanaja, for once, did not show any protest. She was glad that her child would also be fed on breast milk. But this did not translate into gratitude to Kalyanikutty Edathi.

Fourteen

Kalyanikutty Edathi's married life too was a tragedy. Though she had borne a child, and though she had become a mother, she had never known the pleasure of a proper married life that a woman longed for. Menon too had not tried to find out whether she was pleased with her life. The husband had used her mechanically. She had suffered it mechanically. And the result was a child. Their married life had no meaning beyond that. Since Menon had returned from Dubai, it was unlikely that she had even enjoyed the pleasure of a caress. Though they had been married for year, the times when they had sex could be counted on the fingers of a hand. Since he returned from Dubai, Menon only held the title of a husband. He could not perform his other duties. He had lost the ability to do so. There had been days when she had hoped, waited. But if she took the initiative, he would turn away.

Kalyanikutty Edathi did wonder why he behaved like that to her. There was nothing wrong with her. But if ever she approached him, he would say, 'Not today.' That today would never come.

She wondered if the problem was that Menon did not drink like he used to. Perhaps he might have been thinking about Mini. Those thoughts might have made him lonely. Actually, thoughts of Mousumi did not trouble Menon at all. His thoughts were all of Mini. Where would she be? She must have grown up. She must be beautiful. It was unlikely that he would have another child. He had wanted a daughter and that wish would go unfulfilled. That was what made Menon helpless.

But no one recognised how helpless Kalyanikutty Edathi was. Who could she talk to? Once, her old friend Bharathi came to see her when she came home on a holiday. Bharathi's eldest son was studying in a public school in Kodai. The second was in the Sainik school. The third was a girl and she was six years old. Bharathi was lucky. But Kalyanikutty Edathi did not feel jealous. She only thought of her own state.

Bharathi was fairer than when she left the village. Her hair was cut short to shoulder length. She walked around in the village dressed as though she was going to the club in the city where her husband worked. Seeing her walk down the lane in her high heels and dark glasses one of the cheruma boys had run for dear life screaming.

'The foreigner has come.'

'She's walking on stilts.'

'Just look at that bag and those dark glasses and that walk of hers.'

'She's very old. She thinks she won't look her age, if she goes around like this.'

'Who does she think she'll snare if she walks around the village dressed up like this?'

'Women should have a sense of decorum.'

'Her uncle used to call her a fast one in those days.'

'What does it matter? The show is only for the eyes, isn't it?'

'She doesn't wear brassieres.'

'You managed to see that in this time?'

The discussions went on in the houses around.

Bharathi had come alone to see Kalyanikutty Edathi. She had not brought her children. Though Kalyanikutty Edathi would have liked to see the children, she thought that perhaps it was as well that they had not come. She could talk for a while with Bharathi, listen to how her dreams turned out to be true. They had never hidden anything from each other.

'Kalyani, have you decided that one is enough?'

'One is enough. And he can't really do it any longer.'

'That is no problem these days. There are so many things that can be done.'

'He's not willing to go on with the treatment. Each injection costs five hundred rupees. And the next one has to be taken after two days. He took ten of them. I don't think it will work.'

'What about you?'

'There's nothing wrong with me. Most of the time...'

Kalyanikutty Edathi did not feel jealous of Bharathi. At least, she was enjoying herself. Her own life was meant to be lived like this.

Kalyanikutty Edathi went to bed that night thinking of the things that Bharathi had said. She lay close to her husband that night. Not that she was hoping for any reaction. Just that a dream, a wish that something would happen passed before her.

'Why can't you be like Bharathi's husband?' She had wanted to ask that question on some days. She was afraid that if she asked something like that, she would have to put up with the antics of a drunkard. At least now he was lying there quietly, disturbing her only with his snores. He used to drink a lot earlier. Mousumi too would have found him inept when the grip of drink. Kalyanikutty Edathi wondered if that was why she had run away with Johnson. Anyway, there was no point in her hoping for anything. Mousumi could at least run away. Where could she run, from what could she run? Her son was seven years old by now. She could only live out her life like this.

Her son Sankaranarayanan was growing up. She hoped that he would study and become someone. When the boy passed his tenth standard with the best marks in the local school,

Kalyanikutty Edathi felt as though scored she had achieved something. He are hundred per cent in Mathematics and eighty per cent in History. Kalyanikutty Edathi wanted to send him for higher studies. Who would bear the expenses? Her husband no longer had an income. There was no point in hoping that someone else would come forward to help them.

Sankaranarayanan had also recognised that higher education was not meant for him. There was no one for him to ask about what to do next or to advise him. That break from studies turned him off the straight and narrow path.

'He's stopped going to school and spends all his time with some never-do-wells. One always finds him wandering about in the market and places like that.'

'Those boys he hangs around with are bad characters.'

'It seems he has an interest in some girl he studied with.'

'They say she's not a Nair.'

'That of course makes it even better.'

'They say he's started smoking beedies too.'

'It's lucky it isn't drugs.'

Talk about Sankaranarayanan spread like that. Even without his having anything to do with it, he was being propelled in another direction. He would come home at odd times. He did not like talking to anyone. He would sometimes yell at someone at home. But the yelling would not continue long enough for a real fight.

'Sankaranarayanan's ways aren't too good.'

'He'll be spoilt if he's allowed to wander like this in this village.'

'What is to be done?'

'What job can he get here? Where can he be sent?'

He did not come home one day. They thought he would turn up the next day. After a couple of days, they looked him at their relatives' places and his friends' places. No one knew anything.

'He must have run away.'

'He must have eloped with that girl. Who knows?'

But that girl also did not know what had happened to Sankaranarayanan. And the information that he was not to be found did not seem to have moved her in any way at all.

'Shouldn't we look for him?'

'He went of his own will, didn't he? Let him come back when he feels like it.'

'It's not as though he's a small child.'

No one gave any complaint to the police. Everyone prayed that the news would not appear in the newspapers. Such news getting into the newspapers would bring disgrace to the family.

Kalyanikutty Edathi lived amongst these opinions and her own grief at losing her son. She bore the loss by her self. She felt sorry for her son. What was the point in the boy's staying at home? He would have been scolded and cursed by everyone. She did not even have an opportunity to express her own grief.

Years later a news item appeared in one of the papers. A young man had died in a road accident. No one claimed the body. The police traced the young man from a piece of paper in his pocket. The young man who died in a road accident in Assam had been Sankaranarayanan. How did he reach Assam? There was no answer to that question. No one told Kalyanikutty Edathi the news. They were generous enough to think that it would be better for her to continue in the belief that her son was alive somewhere.

Kalyanikutty Edathi would often sit in some corner, away from the eyes of her family, and weep in secret over her lost son. Not that it did any good. She prayed to all the gods she knew to keep her son safe and healthy wherever he was. Kalyanikutty Edathi never found out that her gods had rejected that prayer too.

Her second son Rajasekharan was retarded. The child's brain had been starved of oxygen at the time of birth and that had caused this problem. It had happened because Kalyanikutty Edathi did not get medical help in a difficult labour. If she had been taken to a doctor at the time, this would not have happened. But as usual, the blame for her son's problem was also laid at Kalyanikutty Edathi's door.

'It was lucky that the first also did not end up like this.'

'This was only to be expected.'

'One more burden to the family.'

'This was the only thing that was lacking in the family.'

Rajasekharan was sent to school till he reached the third standard. By that time the family and the school authorities were convinced that there was no point in sending him to school. His body was not fit even for manual labour. Rajasekharan grew big and fat. He had the mental growth of only a three year old when he reached sixteen. All this meant that the boy knew only his mother's affection. He grew up an outsider in his own family. This sorrow was also attributed to Kalyanikutty Edathi's faults.

'One has to give to get.'

'The previous life should have been a good one.'

'What a life this is!'

That was what Kalyanikutty Edathi had to think about herself too. What a life!

Fifteen

It was at noon that the young woman reached the house. She looked about twenty or twenty-one. She wore modern clothes, a pair of jeans and a practically backless top with the neck cut low. She looked healthy and confident. The bag slung over her shoulder was a large one.

'She must be from some troupe of actors.'

'I did hear at the market that a young woman had enquired after someone here.'

'Drama troupes now play a lot in villages.'

'I don't think this is that. This girl is alone.'

'She must have come to write some book or the other. All of them write about villages and make money these days.'

They had heard at the market that morning that a young girl was enquiring about some address in the village. No one would have given her the information.

The strange girl had come to the right house. Most of the people she had asked had not understood the name from the way she pronounced it. That was how she had reached the market. The Panchayat clerk Bhaskaran had to ask her thrice before he could make out what she wanted. The address had to be written down before he could make out which house she meant.

'Oh, Kalyanikutty Amma house. Yes, yes. I come.'

Bhaskaran brought her up to the house, pointed it out saying, 'There house, I go,' and withdrew precipitately. Bhaskaran did not enquire who it was that he had brought to the house. He had liked the way she was dressed and had really wished to enter the house with her. But he felt nervous.

Everyone came out on to the veranda at the arrival of the stranger. All of them looked at her in wonder.

'Kalyanikutty Amma?'

'Yes, yes.'

'I'm so glad.'

There was silence for a while. The stranger did not say anything further. She just stood there wrapped in thought. What was she thinking about? All of them wondered. Her eyes were filling up.

K. N. Menon was fast asleep. He got up and came out when he heard noises outside. He came out because he thought someone was having a problem communicating in English.

The young woman looked at K. N. Menon. Menon too looked at her. No one said anything. Her eyes were just like his eyes, her eyebrows too. It was Kalyanikutty Edathi who realised that. She went nearer to the strange young woman and said, 'Mini.' The rest of the family looked at each other. Each of them was getting an inkling of the truth.

The young woman ran to Menon and hugged him, 'Daddy.'

K. N. Menon too could not control his emotions. 'Mini, Mini...' His eyes were full of tears.

Kalyanikutty Edathi's face had taken on an unusual brightness. She went in and brought a glass of cool water for Mini to drink. Mini was not used to the heat in Kerala. The father and 'mother' sat on either side of the daughter.

Menon again hugged his daughter and wept. No one had expected such a meeting. No one had even dreamt that such a scene would be acted out. The family was wonderstruck.

A daughter who did not know where her father lived or even if he was alive. A father who did not know where his daughter was. The daughter who had been taken away by her mother when she was a small child had sought out her father. Kalyanikutty Edathi was even happier than Menon. She was happy because her husband could regain some of his lost peace of mind with the advent of his daughter.

No one enquired about Mousumi. She had no place there, in this new world. Mini too did not mention her mother. She was so happy that she had found her father in spite of her mother concealing all details about him. She had started this search as soon as she grew up. And she had attained her aim in a village in Kerala. 'I have a father, my father is alive.' Her joy knew no bounds.

Kalyanikutty Edathi accepted Mini as though she had been her own long-lost daughter. The family noticed Kalyanikutty Edathi's unusual brightness and energy. 'This new get-up must be because she does not have a daughter of her own.'

'Probably just to please her husband.'

'Wonder why this young woman had to land up just now.'

'Just to destroy her peace of mind, I suppose.'

As if Kalyanikutty Edathi had peace of mind otherwise.

But it did not feel as though Mini was a stranger in the household. Kalyanikutty Edathi was happy to accept her husband's daughter as her own daughter.

To Mini, everything in this household was strange. She found the lack of a proper bathroom and western-style toilet very difficult to begin with. She did not know how to avoid coming from the bathroom outside the house to her room without wearing her clothes properly. One day, she said she wanted to bathe in the pond. Vanaja went with her. Mini took off all her clothes at the edge of the pond and Vanaja came rushing back. All experiences were new to Mini. She had exhausted the toilet paper she had brought with her. Such things were not available in the village. She realised that others had noticed that she took old newspapers to the toilet outside.

After a couple of days, Mini wanted to go to the temple. She did not know that she had to wear a sari and came out dressed in a clean pair of jeans and a tee-shirt. 'You can't go like this,' the others chorused. All of them were willing to help her wear a sari. Till they came back home from the time they set out for the temple she was afraid to take her hands off her waist in case the sari fell off. Mini did not know that a skirt had to be worn under the sari. She went back inside and borrowed a petticoat which would anchor the sari safely. But she did not feel confident enough to take her hands away from her waist. Even when she stood before the sanctum and prayed, her prayers were mainly that she should not disgrace herself by letting her sari fall off.

When the priest gave her flowers and sandal paste in a leaf, Mini said,

'Thank you'. The priest did not understand what she was saying. Vanaja gave the dakshina to the priest. Mini did not understand that the 'thank you' the priest told Vanaja was a dig at her.

Mini wanted to carry her camera when she went to the temple. 'It isn't really permitted. You can take photographs quietly when the priest turns into the sanctum to do the puja.'

People from the neighbouring houses started dropping in casually. What they all wanted to know was who the new member of the household was. None of them actually asked. They just discussed the newcomer among themselves.

'She must be an artist or writer or something.'

'Don't you remember that other woman came and took a photograph of that untouchable girl who does not wear a blouse.'

'They take all these photographs and sell them for large amounts abroad.'

'Kunjan's daughter Chiruta did not allow that woman to take her photo at first. Then, the woman offered her forty rupees and Chiruta agreed.'

'You get over a thousand rupees for a photograph like that in England.'

'Get lost. What do you know? People there will pose with no clothes at all.'

'But you won't get dark-skinned people. There are plenty of white people there, but not many with dark skins.'

'The Miss World is a dark woman this time. Didn't you read in the newspaper?'

'Did you notice the girl's eyes? Just like Kalyanikutty's husband's eyes.'

'I've heard that he had been married earlier. This girl must be from that marriage. Otherwise they are not going to let her stay there.'

'You are clever. That must be it.'

Though they did not really know the

truth, the villager people decided that the girl was K. N. Menon's daughter. 'The same eyes, the same brows.'

Mini's arrival gave rise to talk not only within the family but the whole village. 'Kalyanikutty need no longer feel sad that she has no daughter.'

'She has the same complexion as that Menon, looks like him too. She must be his daughter.'

'It's not really certain. Why do you cook up things like this?'

'It's not cooking up. She does look like him.'

'Don't talk nonsense. Don't let that poor woman hear you. Let her live in peace. Kalyanikutty Amma has enough problems without adding this as well.'

'Whoever the girl is, she is looking after her like her own daughter.'

'She's a good woman.'

'It's to please her husband.'

'Wonder what language she speaks to the girl in.'

'She spends all her time with Menon anyway.'

'They probably have a lot to tell each other.'

'Kalyanikutty Amma knows enough English to say come, go, sit down, drink this tea and things like that. None of the others in the family know any English.'

'That girl must be feeling stifled.'

'Menon can talk with her, can't he? She talks non-stop anyway.'

'That Adhikari Madhavan Nair's son is a B. A. He went there and tried to talk to the girl.'

'What happened?'

'What happened? He couldn't understand a word of what she said and she couldn't understand a word of what he said. Finally they spoke to each other through gestures.'

'He asked the girl how old she was, I believe. And she got angry and got up and went inside.'

'What's wrong with asking someone how old she is?'

'They say it's not right to ask a girl her age. That's what my husband says. He knows a little about such things.'

'He knows a lot about a lot of things.'

'Don't go too far.'

'Vasu didn't ask her age to marry her or anything, did he? Why did she have to get angry over that?'

'What did it matter to him how old she was?'

'She must be about thirty or thirty two years. It is quite some time since Kalyanikutty got married. Just add the years from there.'

'She doesn't look it, though.'

'Anyway, Kalyanikutty Amma has to look after her as well.'

'Just for a little while, that's all.'

'Menon might ask her to stay back.'

'Not likely. If he does, the rest of the family'll have something to say about that. They won't be as polite as they are now.'

'That's true.'

'When's she going?'

'She doesn't look as though she'll stay here long.'

'Wonder why she's not got married if she's that old.'

'Maybe she didn't get anyone.'

'She's educated, quite good-looking too. So it can't be because she didn't get anyone.'

'Young women have this fashion now, they don't get married in time.'

'She's staying with her mother. They say the new husband is very fond of her.'

All of them looked at each other.

'Don't say such things.'

'Menon will be upset when she leaves.'

'Kalyanikutty Amma too. After she came, Kalyanikutty Amma looks much more cheerful.'

'It's probably because Menon is happier.'

Kalyanikutty Edathi would sometimes go and sit beside them when Menon and Mini talked to each other. Just to listen to the father and daughter speak with each other so happily. But after all the work in the house, such periods of leisure were rare. Menon was also happy to have Kalyanikutty Edathi sit by them while talking to his daughter.

Menon had often wondered why her people treated his wife so badly. She did all the work in the house. She had to take care of everyone. And yet, no one cared about her or sympathised with her. He could not take her to his house. He had not been able to take her with him to his workplace either. Kalyanikutty's life had been tied within the boundaries of this house.

He had even wondered if Kalyanikutty had to suffer so much because she had married him. Once in a while he would think that his fate had become like this because he married Kalyanikutty. Both of them had the same kind of fate.

He had always felt sympathy for her. He had never yelled at her or been rude to her. If he too started behaving like that, what would she do?

He had been very happy when Kalyanikutty Edathi welcomed Mini as though she was her own daughter. Though he himself was separated from his first wife, Mini had been lucky enough to receive affection from two mothers. And Mousumi's new husband too seemed to have treated Mini well. They did not talk of him. They were careful not to mention that name in their discussions.

Menon had often felt like asking Mini about him. But once the topic was inaugurated, Mousumi might enter the conversation. Both of them consciously avoided mentioning either Mousumi or Johnson in their long talks with each other.

Mousumi's life with Johnson had flowed placidly along. Both of them had many interests in common. They would go to the Club practically every evening. They entertained or were entertained by a circle of friends. They had decided earlier on that they did not want children and had been careful to avoid accidents. This helped Johnson treat Mini as his own daughter. Mousumi too paid equal attention to her present husband and her daughter. Mousumi saw Mini as her sole treasure. When Mini started school, Mousumi took up a job, a fairly well-paid one. It did involve travelling, but wasn't too strenuous and it allowed her to get home on time.

Once Mini grew up, the three of them lived together in the house like colleagues or friends. There was no generation gap between them. They would discuss any topic, they would sit and share a drink. Mini had no qualms about smoking in front of Johnson. Nor did Johnson and Mousumi see anything wrong with it. Both of them were careful not to hurt Mini in any way. And so Mini grew up with independent views and habits.

Mini had written to her mother after she reached the village. She did not think about whether her mother would be happy that she had found her father, whether Johnson would like this contact with his wife's first husband or anything. Mini could not help letting her mother know how happy she was to have found her father, in spite of her mother giving her no details about him. After posting the letter, when she thought of all this, Mini consoled herself with the thought that her mother knew her very well and would not be too upset.

Mousumi did not reply. Mini did not expect a reply either. In fact, she had pointedly avoided writing her address. Mini was sure that her mother would have told Johnson about what had happened.

Mini had found her father. What could Mousumi say? She had to be careful not to alienate Mini further. She also had to be careful that this new factor did not disturb the equilibrium that she and her present husband had achieved. Mousumi was decided about that and was careful not to cause disturbances by word or deed.

When Mini was staying with them, Kalyanikutty Edathi's family showed some consideration to Menon. This was not because he was Kalyanikutty Edathi's husband. Once Mini left, things went back to the old stage. He had always been an outsider there.

He could never spend some time peacefully with his wife. She hardly had time after all the housework. Or, if on a rare occasion, she found some time, there would be a lot of comments about that.

'Look at them flirting away in that corner.'

'They've forgotten how old they are.'

'Wonder what they find so much to say to each other.'

'She's normally not very talkative.'

'But you should see her giggling and talking with her husband.'

'Don't they have any sense of shame?'

'They got married rather late, didn't they? Let them enjoy themselves.'

'She must be finding all this new.'

'But it isn't new to him.'

'He's lived like the white men.'

Menon was never treated like Vanaja's and Soudamini's husbands.

When Mini was there, Menon would sit on the outside veranda, smoking his endless cigarettes, wrapped in thought. That too caused comments.

'Wonder who he's dreaming of.'

'Must be his old wife.'

'He must be getting depressed at the thought of his daughter going back.'

'That must be it.'

'He knows she can't stay here permanently. So what's the point in being depressed?'

'He's seeing his daughter after a long while, isn't he? Someone else took her away, isn't it?'

One day, Thekkedath Meenakshi Amma asked Kalyanikutty Edathi, 'This is that girl, isn't it? Don't worry Kalyanikutty.' She did not wait for Kalyanikutty Edathi's reply. 'Don't worry Kalyanikutty, she seems to be a nice girl. You don't have a daughter anyway. Just think this is the daughter given by god.'

Kalyanikutty Edathi listened to all the comments. She did not reply or respond in any manner.

No one asked Mini when she planned to return. Kalyanikutty Edathi would have liked her to stay for a long while. She was happy in her husband's happiness and the change that had come over him since Mini came. She was also worried over what would happen once Mini went back.

The comments continued even after Mini left.

'She's finally gone. Kalyanikutty can heave a sigh of relief.'

'What relief! She looked happier when the girl was here. She's looking haggard again.'

'Wonder when she'll come back.'

'I don't think she'll come back. She must have got fed up of the village. She wouldn't have liked the ways of this place, I'm sure.'

'It's the first time she's seeing her father as far as she can remember. She's seen him. Why should she come again? She'll stick on with her mother. I don't think she's going to look this side again.'

'I don't suppose her mother'll send her again either. She didn't bring her up all these years just to let her go now.'

Sixteen

Mini's journey in search of her father was an epic. Her mother Mousumi had not told her anything about her father. Mini was not even sure that her father was still alive. Her mother disliked being questioned about her father. Though she had asked questions earlier, she stopped after she grew a little. She did not see any point in doing what her mother disliked. She grew up in her mother's shade.

Mini did not like calling her mother's husband a stepfather. Though he had always treated her as his own daughter, Mini always felt he was just a good friend of her mother's and hers. As she grew older this friendship strengthened.

Mini had felt lonely at first. But she waited till she grew up and could stand on her own feet before she examined those feelings. Johnson had not felt as though

Mini was his own daughter. He did not see her as a stepdaughter either. He thought of her as a young girl who grew up in his house. Her stay there had not caused any problem. Mini too was a quiet child, creating no problem at all.

Johnson sent Mini to Paris to study. Since he did not have other children, there was no barrier to his doing all that was necessary for her. Johnson and Mousumi had visited Mini in Paris before she graduated.

It was when she was studying in Paris that Mini developed an interest in painting. She became involved in studying art and learnt to appreciate art critically. Mini would have liked to spend a few more years in Paris. But she did not want to live away from her mother for more years. Her mother too could not think of being without her daughter for more years. Mousumi saw security in her daughter's presence. So, Mini returned to India with her mother and Johnson.

The problem was where they should

settle. Neither Johnson nor Mousumi liked the idea of returning to Pune. The city with its old memories was ruled out immediately. Mousumi liked crowded and lively Bombay. But Johnson did not like the idea of its fast pace. Finally, both of them decided on Bangalore as a suitable place of settling down.

Once she returned to India, Mini felt even more interested in tracing her father. She would seek him out if he was still alive. She set out on her quest with the meagre particulars that she had. As she travelled around, she would ask all the Malayalis she met whether they knew a K. N. Menon from Calicut. She did not receive any answers. She did not even know her father's proper name or the name of his family. She was sure she would not be able to locate him with the little that she knew. Still, Mini did not give up. She did not let Johnson or Mousumi know about her search for her father, since she did not know how they would react to it. If they knew and objected, she would be forced to abandon the search even before it was properly started. So she continued her questions and search secretly. Though she was busy with other activities, she did not abandon her quest.

Mini was interested in theatre. When she was working for her degree in Paris, she had tried to learn about the theatre as well. There had been opportunities to meet directors of repute and to talk about drama. Mini had grown to like Bernard whom she met at a lot of these get-togethers. They used to meet once in a while.

One day, Bernard came out with what was in his mind, 'Mini, I want...'

Mini did not let him complete the sentence, 'If you have any such idea my friend, get rid of it immediately.'

Bernard remained silent for a while. This girl who sat before him was a new and unfamiliar Mini. What could he say? It was Mini who broke the lengthening silence.

'My friend,' The way she addressed him was also unexpected. There wasn't much friendship in it, more a kind of harshness. 'There's no point in keeping such ideas in your mind. My mother married a foreigner and accepted his lifestyle as her own. I don't blame her for that. But I want to live as an Indian.'

'How can our relationship prevent that?'

'Bernard, you would not understand even if I tried to explain that. Especially since you are of mixed blood yourself. Let's not talk of that. Let us remain friends.'

Mini met Bernard a number of times after that. One day he said, 'I'm getting married.'

'Congratulations! Who's she?'

'You know Claire who's studying Mohiniattam here, she's the girl.'

'I see.'

What could Mini say? Mini had

nothing to say. She only felt that the stand she'd taken when Bernard had proposed had been right. Bernard did not see his future in Indian Theatre, but somewhere else. After some time, Claire returned to France. And Bernard did not say anything about her after that.

I had met Mini accidentally at an exhibition of paintings in the city. One day we were walking along together and had gone to a café for a cup of coffee. Chatting idly over the coffee, she spoke of her family and I realised that Mini's father had to be from my area. I also realised that he was probably related to me. But I didn't inform Mini of my conclusions then.

I spent that whole night thinking over whether I should tell Mini what I had guessed. After all, it involved the life of two families. Letting out a small fact could elicit any sort of response from them. It might destroy the peace of the two families for ever. What would Mini say if I said that I was acquainted with her father? What would be Kalyanikutty Edathi's reaction to the entry of Mini into her life? Suppose she asked me why I had interfered? Mini was searching for her father. People might ask why I had to go and volunteer the information. But since I knew the whole story, it seemed wrong not to let her know.

Weeks passed. I used to meet Mini, go along for walks once in a while. I'd often been on the point of telling her the truth. Each time, I held back just in time.

After a few weeks, I had gone to the village. I told Kalyanikutty Edathi about Mini. I told her in secret. 'Kalyanikutty Edathi, I want to tell you something. Don't misunderstand my motives. You needn't even tell your husband if you don't want to. But I can't hide this any longer.' I started with this long introduction. After a long silence with me trying to organise what I had to say, I said, 'I've seen Mini.'

I did not add anything immediately, but watched Kalyanikutty Edathi's face.

I didn't see shock or irritation there. There wasn't a rush of happiness either. I could not make a guess of how she had taken the news. After a while, Kalyanikutty Edathi asked for more details. Where did I meet her and the rest of it. I explained about Mini's search for her father. As soon as she had reached India after her studies she had started her search. We had met by accident. While talking of all sorts of subjects, this quest of hers had also come up.

'Does she look like her father?' Kalyanikutty Edathi had a smile on her face when she asked.

The atmosphere lightened with that. 'Why don't you see for yourself?' I gathered up my courage and asked, 'Shall I tell her to come here and see you all?' I had not told Mini anything. I'd not told her even that her father was alive or where he lived. I'd decided that I would do whatever Kalyanikutty Edathi wanted me to do.

Her reply came quickly, 'Let her

come and stay here for a few days. It'll make her father happy. And I'm sure no one here will have any objection.'

How could Kalyanikutty Edathi take such a bold decision? Had she forgotten the circumstances in which she lived? But she seemed quite decided when she said that. As though she would face any opposition when it came. It was the first time I was seeing this side of Kalyanikutty Edathi. Of course she would have been sure of her husband's support. And she was ready to face the objections of the others.

After I got back to Bangalore and rejoined work, I met Mini again. As usual we went for a walk in the evening and went to the usual café.

'Whom did you meet during your leave? What is the news from home?'

I did not start with a long introduction. I felt it would be better to enter straight into the subject. How long could I bear the burden of this unshared knowledge? Mini had not suspected that I might have the information she wanted and so she had shown no curiosity about my village and family. She had not expected me to provide the clue. I thought it would not be proper to prolong this secrecy.

'Mini, I have something to tell you. Don't be shocked. I had been planning to tell you this for some time.'

Mini just sat gazing at me, unaware of what was to come.

'I know your father. You might even say we are related.'

Mini sat silently for a short while and then started sobbing. Her father was alive. The joy of seeing someone who actually knew her father flowed out through her tears. I was rather embarrassed because this was such a public place. When Mini had got over her shock, we continued talking.

'Tell me everything. I want to hear every last detail. I want to know about my father's family, about his wife, about his other children.' Mini was in a hurry now.

'Come, let's go sit where there isn't such a crowd.' Mini's shower of questions continued after we reached the park.

'Mini, Kalyanikutty Edathi was very pleased to hear about you. They're waiting for you.'

'Truly?' Mini could not believe her ears.

'Shall I let them know that you would like to visit them?'

That was how Mini reached the village.

Seventeen

Mini stayed only a fortnight in the village. Menon started getting depressed at the thought of the coming parting days before she actually left. He did not show it overtly. His daughter was going to her mother. There was no way he could tell her not to go to the mother who had brought her up. He knew he had no right to. He could not even ask her to stay for some more days. After all, this was not his house. He did not ask his daughter what her mother's life with her second husband was like. He did not want to know about that life either. He could even feel some sort of gratitude for the fact that his daughter had been so well looked-after by her step-father.

He had forgiven Mousumi for eloping with Johnson. But he was unable to forgive her for taking Mini away from him. Mini did not speak to Kalyanikutty Edathi about her mother. She acknowledged who Kalyanikutty Edathi was, gave her the respect due. Kalyanikutty Edathi too did not expect anything other than that Mini would make her father happy while she was there.

The day before Mini left Menon smoked cigarette after cigarette. Though the doctor had told him that he had to control his smoking, that day Menon did not obey those instructions. He would usually lie down for a while after lunch. Kalyanikutty Edathi noticed that the conversations that the father and daughter used to have in the evenings had become shorter. She did not say anything. Nor did she try to console either of them.

Mini picked up her things and set off. She had bought a palm leaf umbrella, the type without a handle that is worn like a hat. The kind of thing that farm labourers wore as they worked in the fields. Mini had fallen for it. The problem was transporting it. 'I'll carry it in my hand.' They were afraid that a long farewell would become too emotional. Mini just said, 'I'm going.' Menon hugged his daughter. Kalyanikutty Edathi put both her hands on the girl's head and blessed her.

'You'll come again, won't you?' Kalyanikutty Edathi's words rang out. Menon was doubtful whether Mini would come again. He wished he could be sure of seeing her again. But he did not speak of his wishes. Nor did he build up hopes. Mini vanished from sight.

Would Mousumi give permission for another trip like this when she came to know what her daughter had done? What would be her reaction to this? Menon thought about it but could not find an answer.

Mini did not get a chance to see her father again. The day Mini returned, Johnson told Mousumi, 'We have a fairly contented life. Don't forget that.'

The next night Mousumi told Mini, 'Don't forget one thing, my dear. I have no one else. I want to live in peace. Don't disturb things, will you?' Mousumi was trying to control her emotions.

She had seen her father. She had found out that her father was alive, and what sort of a man he was. She had attained what she had set out to do. Her intention had been only to see her father. She had not planned to live permanently with him or to reunite her mother and father or anything of the sort. She had lost the feeling that she did not have a father. Just the feeling that she did have a father was a new one to her.

Mini decided that she would not destroy the peace of two families. She had set out on an adventurous journey and that journey had reached its destination. She was content. It was all very like a dream. She tore up the diary that she had written when she stayed with her father. One could tear up what was written on paper. But her mind would not forget. She did not know how long a period would have to pass before the pictures of those days vanished from her mind.

After getting back to Bangalore, Mini got in touch with Kalyanikutty Edathi's relatives who lived in Bangalore. She wanted to see more of them, find out about her father's family. It was this hope that impelled her to get in touch with those people. She introduced some of them to her mother and Johnson.

'I'm not coming to meet anyone. No one need come here mentioning that connection,' was the reaction of one of the distant relatives.

'They created a child and then left her and went away.'

'But what did the girl have to do with that?'

'Whatever, I don't want to get involved with those people.'

I met Mini again at that old restaurant. Two years after she had gone to the village and come back, Mini rang me again.

'We'll meet at that old place.'

We met at the restaurant at the time fixed earlier. Mini seemed happier than before.

'Thank you, I'm really obliged to you. If you hadn't helped me, I wouldn't have been able to meet my father. It was my life's wish to meet him. I really feel fulfilled.'

'More at peace with yourself?'

'Still, you could have told me all this when you first got to know me.'

'I had to consider more than one point of view. I didn't know how Kalyanikutty Edathi's people would receive you. That's why I didn't mention this earlier.'

'She's such a good woman. But...' Mini did not complete the thought.

'But what? Tell me.'

'Everybody exploits her. Are all your people like this?'

'Every household has people like

that. Think of the people you know, Mini.'

'That's true.'

There were people like that in Mousumi's family as well. Mini's mother had grown up with a lot of freedom and had even chosen to lead the life she wanted. Her elder sister had married a man high up in the burcaucratic hierarchy. Later, he went abroad. Mini thought of Gouri. Gouri's place in her family was the equivalent of Kalyanikutty Edathi's in hers. Gouri too functioned like a machine in a household, ensuring the comforts of others. Mousumi had not gone back to her tharavad after she married Johnson. Gouri was spending a life uselessly in that big house.

'What are you thinking of, Mini?'

'Nothing in particular. Just that what you said now was true.'

'There are people like this everywhere.'

As far as Kalyanikutty Edathi was concerned, some pleasant days had passed as an interlude in her cursed life. She did not even know whether they were true or just dreams. Mini had behaved so affectionately to her? And her husband had been so alive when his daughter was there. She had seen a different face of her usually morose husband those days. Was that the real face. Human life and relationships passed, rising and falling with dreams and their destruction . What could creatures like her expect from that?

There was an Ummam tree near the gatehouse. Mini was attracted by that flowering tree. When she returned from the village, she carried a picture of that tree full of flowers in her mind. She had also picked up a bit of esoteric knowledge. That the smell of Ummam flowers would intoxicate women. Mini did not experiment. But she had brought seeds from the tree. Another thing that attracted her was the way the middle-aged men wore their mundus. She could not make out why they wore their mundus below their navels. Wouldn't it be firmer if tied above the navel? She felt that the way the men wore the mundu beat the way modern girls wore their clothes.

Mini had travelled once by the local bus. No one sat near her. She wouldn't have minded if they did. But if she told one of the men that he could sit next to her, they might have taken it as an invitation. She could not understand the way the minds of the people in the village worked. But she could feel the eyes of the passengers move over her from head to foot as long as she was in the bus. Mini went only once by bus.

She had taken photographs too. Photographs of the different faces of the village and the villagers. Festivals, ponds and their steps, temples, labourers in the field, the mason dressing red stone, workers using a saw to split a log, women clad in wet clothes on their way to the temple, old men with no teeth and sunken cheeks, the huge banyan tree which gave shade to the village, the school anniversary, political meetings, weddings, rice cooking in large copper vessels, the ada for the payasam being cut into small pieces with chisels, death anniversary rituals and so on. Some of them were so good that they could have been exhibited. Johnson even suggested that an exhibition be arranged. Mousumi did not say anything. The photographs remained a secret hoard in Mini's albums.

K. N. Menon died soon after Mini came and went. It was more a disease of the mind than of the body. When they found that he could not swallow at all and this state continued for four or five days, he was taken to the hospital. He had ulcers in the stomach. There wasn't much expert help available and no effort was made to arrange for an expert opinion. He threw up a lot of blood just before he died. So Kalyanikutty Edathi became a widow.

The doctor should have been called in when he started getting such severe stomach pain. The family didn't think it necessary.

Kalyanikutty Edathi had suggested

that a doctor be called in. 'Call a doctor for an ordinary stomach pain! What nonsense. Just mix a little crushed ginger in lime juice and give it a few times. Just two doses and the pain will go away.'

When the pain became really severe, Damodaran Master was called in. Damodaran Master would dispense homeo medicines. He'd learnt homeopathy from books. When he retired from his job as school master he started concentrating more on homeopathy. Damodaran Master always claimed that homeopathy had a medicine for every person and every illness. He would give medicines to anyone who approached him and did not accept any fees.

'That Narayanan Nair could not control his temper earlier. He improved so much after taking Damodaran Master's medicine.'

'But he's still very hot-tempered.'

'He stopped taking the medicine half-way through. Also you have to follow a diet very strictly. You aren't supposed to drink tea or coffee and things like that.'

'He's stopped taking tea and coffee. But every evening, he needs a dram or two of...'

'How will he get better then? What's the point in blaming Damodaran Master?'

It was Gopalan who said that when Kunhukuttiamma had prolonged labour pains, she had taken some medicine given by Damodaran Master and had delivered immediately.

'Master's hand is a lucky hand.'

But the medicine did not work for K. N. Menon. The second day, Damodaran Master took out some small pills and mixed some of them with a white liquid from a bottle.

'Let him take six of these pills in the morning and evening. He'll feel better.'

Menon, however did not get better.

Kalyanikutty Edathi started getting really worried. The rest of the family did not seem to be very worried. They were of the opinion that homeopathy medicines took time to act.

The third day, Menon started feeling choked and giddy. It was almost a coma.

'He'd better be taken to the hospital.'

'How can he be taken in this state?'

All of them looked at each other. Getting involved would mean spending money.

'This isn't the time to think of anything else. Before he's worse,...'

Menon was taken to the hospital with the help of the neighbours.

More than her husband's death, it was the thought that she would have to face the indignity of the ostracism that being a widow entailed. K. N. Menon was buried in the compound away from the house. No one came from his family.

'Sankaranarayanan will not be able to reach. He is on tour.'

Kalyanikutty Edathi did not know whom to tell so that Mini would get to know the news. She consoled herself with the thought that she herself could write a little later.

It was one of those days after her husband's death that the thunderbolt fell on her ears. Someone was speaking of her, 'It must be that accursed female who did that.' She did not understand what she was supposed to have done. No one told her either. They had decided that she was a curse on the family. She had heard all sorts of epithets applied to herself. And had borne all of them. But she could not bear being called the accursed one.

If she had been accursed, they could have cast her out. She was not coward enough to commit suicide though. A life which did not mean anything.

The term accursed continued to echo in her ears. Her health too started deteriorating. Kalyanikutty Edathi was slowly, slowly, becoming good for nothing, unable to do anything, a body without even health...

Kalyanikutty Edathi was no longer able to do the housework. She'd lost her appetite too. She would go and sit on the veranda every now and then while she worked. If she slept off there, there would be comments on that. Even when she sat there, unable to get up and work, they would call for her. To say that she could not go was unthinkable.

'Imagine lying like a buffalo in this bright daylight.'

'Just like her.'

'What's wrong with her anyway?'

No one asked what had happened, why she was lying down, whether she was ill.

'Anyone would feel tired once in a while. There's nothing to talk about in that.'

Even as she lay down, no one paid any attention to her. No one realised that she was getting thinner and weaker day by day.

One day, she did not get up to pull up the drinking water from the well. When someone went to find out what had happened, her breathing seemed laboured. Everyone gathered round.

'It's nothing. Don't bother,' was all she said. Those were the last words she spoke.

Kalyanikutty Edathi had not expected anyone to bother about her throughout her life.

She did not know how to explode in anger or melt in tears. She spent a whole lifetime without expecting any attention. Even as she stopped breathing, she was happy that she had not been tied to the bed by a long illness.

'It happened suddenly,' wrote Kumarettan. Lucky for Kalyanikutty Edathi. If she had been bedridden for some time, she would have been cursed even for that. 'She did not have to lie in bed with any illness.' They would not have thought she was lucky not to be ill. They would have considered themselves lucky that they had got rid of the accursed one.

I did not reply to Kumarettan. What could I write? Kalyanikutty Edathi was lucky that she had an easy death. Her soul was not going to find its salvation by the prayers of the family. What they had lost was only the accursed one of the family.

How could lives be like this? That question about Kalyanikutty Edathi remained. She had served everyone as well as she could, had done backbreaking tasks, made all sacrifices and still had suffered everyone's contempt. The question was really about the lives around her.

Kalyanikutty Edathi had had dark marks under her eyes even in her teens. This had been called a lack of luck, the mark of a curse. No one had understood that the tears that had not been shed had gathered there and caused that mark.